When You
Castrate Me

Sandra Athena

WHEN YOU CASTRATE ME

iUniverse books may be ordered through booksellers or by contacting:

iUniverse
1663 Liberty Drive
Bloomington, IN 47403
www.iuniverse.com
1-800-Authors (1-800-288-4677)

Because of the dynamic nature of the Internet, any web addresses or links contained in this book may have changed since publication and may no longer be valid. The views expressed in this work are solely those of the author and do not necessarily reflect the views of the publisher, and the publisher hereby disclaims any responsibility for them.

Any people depicted in stock imagery provided by Thinkstock are models, and such images are being used for illustrative purposes only. Certain stock imagery © Thinkstock.

ISBN: 978-1-5320-1010-1 (sc)
ISBN: 978-1-5320-1035-4 (e)

Print information available on the last page.

iUniverse rev. date: 10/29/2016

This book is dedicated to a very good friend of mine. The leaves of the tree may wither, the season may change, and my last name may be replaced. Come what may, you will be forever treasured in my mind, heart and soul. My handsome dear friend, Matthew Andersen, here's my promise. This story is for you.

PROLOGUE

"WHERE have you been?!?"

He heard her yelling at him. She's throwing out things at him again just as he expected.

"Laura, wait-". Before he could even speak a word a lampshade almost hit his face.

"I have been sitting here a hundred years waiting for you!"

She's exaggerating again.

"Look, I texted you. Don't wait for me since I will be going home late. I tried to call you. But-"

PAK!

She slapped him. Didn't even let him finish his sentence. Then she gave him a punch in the face again.

Shit!

He had enough of her being abusive.

He had enough of this thing called 'love'.

He pushed her to the wall and was about to punch her on the face when his son cried.

His son. He is exactly his carbon copy.

Laura is his girlfriend. He planned to marry her. They are living together in this apartment for almost a year now.

She always beat him. If there's a battered wife, there's also a battered husband and that's him.

But he's not blind anymore. She doesn't love him. She just stayed by his side for financial security and support for their child.

But enough is enough.

He can't stand her attitude anymore.

"I want you to leave, Laura! Leave and never come back!" He shouted at her. Didn't even pay a little attention to the crying child in their bedroom.

"How dare you throw me out of this house!" She shouted back at him.

"This is my house!"

"I am not leaving without my son!" She said.

"Fine. Bring the child with you for all I care! And don't you ever show your face again!"

He vowed. Never will I fall in love again! Never will I lost myself to a woman again! Never!

PROLOGUE

"WHERE have you been?!?"

He heard her yelling at him. She's throwing out things at him again just as he expected.

"Laura, wait-". Before he could even speak a word a lampshade almost hit his face.

"I have been sitting here a hundred years waiting for you!"

She's exaggerating again.

"Look, I texted you. Don't wait for me since I will be going home late. I tried to call you. But-"

PAK!

She slapped him. Didn't even let him finish his sentence. Then she gave him a punch in the face again.

Shit!

He had enough of her being abusive.

He had enough of this thing called 'love'.

He pushed her to the wall and was about to punch her on the face when his son cried.

His son. He is exactly his carbon copy.

Laura is his girlfriend. He planned to marry her. They are living together in this apartment for almost a year now.

She always beat him. If there's a battered wife, there's also a battered husband and that's him.

But he's not blind anymore. She doesn't love him. She just stayed by his side for financial security and support for their child.

But enough is enough.

He can't stand her attitude anymore.

"I want you to leave, Laura! Leave and never come back!" He shouted at her. Didn't even pay a little attention to the crying child in their bedroom.

"How dare you throw me out of this house!" She shouted back at him.

"This is my house!"

"I am not leaving without my son!" She said.

"Fine. Bring the child with you for all I care! And don't you ever show your face again!"

He vowed. Never will I fall in love again! Never will I lost myself to a woman again! Never!

MEET ALEXIS

*W*OW!

It's just one of his regular nights. He is enjoying his drink while sitting prominently on one of the chairs in his club. Their club actually. He and his friends started this business two years ago when he arrived in this foreign land.

To him it was just a whisper. But it seemed that she heard it because now she is smiling seductively at him.

He's talking about the sexy, skinny, petite woman standing across the counter. He's just sitting opposite to the counter and he can tell that she's sexy.

She's not his type though, he doesn't feel the same familiar sparks. But he is sad tonight and swear to heavens this woman will going to fill his lonely night.

"Hi, handsome!" He could see that she almost winked at him when he walked towards her.

"Hello, young lady. Nice boobs." He stared at her big breasts. With her size he wonders how heavy each piece would be. They look angry and trying to escape from her over-fitted halter tops. He can't help but smile of his crazy thoughts.

"Want to touch it?" Again with that alluring smile while she softly touch his chest with her finger.

He quickly drink the last drop of his wine and grab her breasts like he just won in a bingo game.

And oh, they are not fake. Indeed, they're big and soft. She must be size 34 cup C. Well, he's an expert when it comes to breasts sizes.

"So, want to suck them? They are yours." She said. She liked what he's doing. She even moan a little.

Then he put his hands inside her top wear. Well, the nipples feel good.

"My apartment is located nearby." She said again.

"Let's go to my car." He told her instead. She followed him without hesitation.

When they reached his car he sit on the car's hood and he had her sit on his lap. He slowly undressed her and suck each nipple like a hungry beast. She's like a crazy bitch who moaned loudly.

He slowly slid his hand inside her miniskirt. She's wearing a lace panty he's sure of it. He had slept with 27 women and knows all of them panty types. Then he found her cherry. Oh how she like the cherry of petite women, just like his favorite cherry apple cake desert their cute flower never made him lost his appetite.

"Oh, please touch my V baby." She sounds like begging.

And he is the generous kind.

He slid his index finger inside her hole while his thumb is touching her clit. Then he slid the middle finger and he finger fuck her using his index and middle fingers.

"Oh, shit, fuck me more!" She cursed.

He continued to finger fuck her. Then he felt her hand touching his crouch. He is still not hard.

What's happening to him?

"Goodness! You're big but you're not hard." She looked surprise with his size but a little annoyed upon knowing that he is not hard yet.

"Can you do something to wake 'him' up?" He asked her.

"Sure." She willingly heed him.

He stand and she's the one sitting on the hood now.

She slowly pull 'him' out from his pants. His property, his pride. It looks like it had just awakened from a hundred years of sleep. She slowly suck him. She's giving 'him' a good blow.

It took her almost 10 minutes to wake 'him' up. Then he slowly fuck her with his big dick.

Just the same way he suck her nipples she also moans even louder after he enters her.

She's screaming someone else's name. If this is the woman he loves he could have slapped her by now. But love? The hell he care.

"I believe there's true love forever."

That familiar line.

Shit!

He could feel his orgasm and he's cumming.

Shit!!

Another curse.

He's been cursing a lot because of this woman.

He cum on her face.

Then he left her.

"My name is Leila." The woman shouted just when he turned his back on her.

But he never looked back.

He will go home very quick and check his laptop.

What's happening to him? He missed her.

Oh, Casslynn.

CASSLYNN, "THE AUTHOR"

"**H**OW are you doing, *ganda* (his term for beauty)?"

She's trying to finish the last two chapters of her book as her editor needs it for the next month's release. She was engrossed in writing and almost knock her butt upon receiving the message.

It was Andrew.

That jerk.

She met him a week ago in FindSome. It's one of the famous dating site of today. Yeah, she's into online dating. She has a secret dream, a fantasy for her future. Sadly, looks like all those dreams can only become real in her stories.

She gave a loud sigh before she turn her attention back to the computer screen.

"Yes?" She typed her reply and pressed the send button.

"I missed you. Are you busy?" He replied.

"Nah. I just finished my work. I missed you, too.... I missed your perfectly beautiful manhood." She replied and sent a blushing smiley.

He replied with an inlove smiley.

If she's easy to fool with, she may have believed him. But no, Andrew had been honest to her from the beginning and he is not the type who believes in love.

"I wish you're here *ganda* so I can hug and kiss you." He said without hesitation.

She knows he's joking. And she is in the mood today to play with him.

"Let's meet up then."

"I'm not into date, *ganda*. I would want to see you though."

"Are you afraid? It's just going to be a friendly date or if you call it a date. Are you scared of falling for me?"

She sounded like she's seducing him.

"Ha ha. No, I know myself better. I wish you can castrate me now and I will be in complete surrender under your power."

"Then let's meet up. Do you know that no man can resist me? And you're not an exception."

"I know you're a beauty. But nada, I will never fall in love. I'm sick of relationships."

"I can heal you. My sexy legs can do so much." She sounded like a charming, cheap now. But she's just trying to make him get out of his shell.

"Oh my balls." She could feel he's chuckling. He continues. **"I would love to hang your legs in the air while exploring you underneath with my mouth and tongue."**

"Will I get the chance to touch your perfect, enormous source of life down there?" Now she's getting far and having hard time to stop herself.

"Yes, master *ganda*. And I am giving you the full control of my balls. You can slap them, cut them and do anything with them."

"You're crazy." She sent him a laughing smiley. **"What are you going to do with my cherry pop pop then?"**

"I would touch your precious flower, first with my thumb, then with my tongue."

Shit! She feel wet. What kind of conversation is this, all full of filthy things.

"Hmmm. We're getting far. I don't want you to rape me in your mind. Ha ha." She stopped herself before she can commit any sin.

"Yeah." He sent a sad, crying smiley. But just like a car's gear he easily switched to another topic. **"Do you know that I fucked a hottie chick earlier on the hood of my car?"**

"Yuck! That's so cheap." She suddenly feel a little pain. **"How old is she?"** She asked him, without entertaining the little feeling of jealousy inside her.

"Nah. Don't know. Can't even remember her name."

"Wow. How can you just forget the name of the woman you slept with?"

"I can't always remember."

She was speechless. He's always very vocal of wanting to have sex with her. So what is her difference to these women he slept with? Will he forget her name, too? She was staring at nothing for few minutes.

"Are you still there, *ganda*?"

Just then she was back to reality.

"Yes. I'm thinking of writing a book about you." Her tongue slipped.

"Wow, that's so sexy. Really? You're a writer?"

God! What have she done? She can't tell him about her profession. No one should know.

"I'm a novelist."

She told him. She has no choice. She's not good at lying. Anyway, nothing to be afraid of, she doesn't really have any plan to meet him in person.

"Awesome! When can you write a book for me?"

What did she get herself into? Can she really write a romance book for him? To someone like him who is playing with love?

"Let me come up with a good title first. Give me a moment." She changed her status to away. But not to think of a title for a book she will write for him. She send the last two chapters of her book to her editor. Em has been bugging her to finish this book. Because she's only using a wifi her Internet is a little bit slow and so it took her couple of minutes to send her mail. She change her status back to online.

"Hey, I'm back."

"I'm here. So..?"

"Yeah, I think yours will be my next book."

"Great. So what will it be?"

"I can't think of a plot for now. Can you give me a little idea of what kind of book you want me to write for you?"

For the first time in her life she didn't have an idea of what to write. What kind of love story would fit to someone like Andrew? Just then something popped up her mind. "How about writing something about castration?"

"Wow. That's even great!"

"Yes, it will be a great story since I am the writer. It will hit big in the market." She sent him a smiley that winked.

"Hmm.. *Ganda*....."

"Yes?"

"Why don't you give me your sweetest kiss?" He suddenly changed the topic.

"Hmm.. My lips would love to give you a little bite."

"Ohh. Can I have a French kiss?"

She sent him a hugging smiley instead.

"Mmmmm that was good. My French kiss?"

"Yes, handsome. But not now, I need to go away for a while. Need to run some errand." A good escape.

"Oh, alright." He sounded disappointed. **"I will miss you, beauty."**

"Take care, Andrew." Her reply.

Then she exit the chat screen but his last reply caught her eyes. And surprised her.

"No, baby, my name is Alexis. Alexis Isaiah Andrews."

Chapter 1

"HEY, bro. We're planning to go somewhere out of town next weekend."

He heard him saying they will be out this weekend.

"And what do you guys plan to do? Close our business when its weekend that customers are rushing in?" Irritated. He asked.

He had a bad day. It's almost a week now and Casslynn is not responding to any of his chat messages in Netto and FindSome. He's going crazy thinking she might be chatting with someone else now.

SHIT!

What is he thinking? Casslynn is just another woman.

His friend Robert is staring at him while thinking what has gotten into his friend. Rob is a friend and partner in this business.

"Bro, I didn't say this weekend, I said NEXT weekend. What's happening with you? How's the place there look like?" He smiled.

"What?!" He asked not sure what he mean but he sounded pissed now.

"You're spaced out, bro. Are you in love?" He sounded like teasing him.

He felt his face getting hot.

"Of course not! I have no sex for one week now and that made me upset." That was a good alibi. But HELL! Him? In love? He doesn't even know what love is.

Just then another friend came in.

"Oh, there you are. Hey guys, I would like you to meet my friends."

He is with two women. His guess is that he found them in the street. They look like whores. Wearing such skimpy clothes. The only thing that caught his attention is the other woman. She's petite with nice legs.

He just glared at Franky giving him a questioning look. Which Franky completely ignores.

"Well, bro, this is Ada." The petite one. Franky gave him a wink. His friend knows his type and weakness. "And this is Brenda." He introduced the other woman.

He doesn't care about their names he would forget them anyway.

"Andrew." He said to the petite woman.

Yes, he always give girls his last name which he changed from Andrews to Andrew. Only Casslynn knows his real name. What had gotten into him why he did that, he doesn't have any idea. Maybe because he doesn't really have any plan to see her in person.

Speaking of Casslynn. What is she doing right now? Seems that she forgot him already.

"I'm married." He smiled at how Rob introduced himself. Every time they try him to meet a woman he always say he's married instead of giving his name.

Rob is afraid of his wife. That's what he thought. Rob is 42 and is married to a 28-year old woman and they have two kids.

One thing he hates about marriages, he hated the idea of someone nagging at him. Controlling him. Demanding him to do something. And he can't stand having sex with just one woman every day.

"Oh, guys, I need to go to the counter now and assist Ben. So, you enjoy, okay?" Rob said while giving him a wink before walking towards the counter.

And without a second, Franky left with the other woman. Which name he already forget. He knows Franky will bring the woman to somewhere private. He was left with the petite woman, Myra, ah Amanda... whatever.

Shit!

He's so bad with names. Especially when his mind is occupied with something, he easily forget names.

But you never forget Casslynn's name.

The other part of his brain said. He didn't pay attention to it.

"Hey, Andrew, do you have any girlfriend?" 'Any'. So this woman is expecting him to have multiple girlfriends.

"No, I don't." That was honest.

"Good. Can we go out?" Then she slowly cling into him. Giving him a smack on the lips.

He's not surprise. Women of this kind normally fall in his charm. No sweat, he'll get them.

"Hmmm." He touched her butt. It's sexy enough. And the boobs are great. "I know a place. Let's go." She excitedly followed him.

He will have a good fucking session tonight.

*****

THE woman is a great performer in bed.

She give his big gun little bites after licking 'him', while touching his balls.

Ughhhh.

"Do you have any plan to enter me?" She asked him.

Yes, they had been doing foreplays for almost an hour now. He doesn't understand why he can't fuck this woman. Sure he finger fuck her. But with her big shaft, he's not getting any interest.

"I will bring you home. Go and change now, Mandy."

PAK!

She slapped him.

"My name is Ada, not Andy, not Amanda, not Mandy!" She yelled at her. "And don't bother. I know how to get home. I don't need a lame man like you!" Then she hurriedly pick up her clothes and left.

Whew!

How many times did he get slap by women simply because he called them wrong names.

Will Casslynn slapped her, too, in case he forgot her name?

Can she just castrate him instead?

He's having a vision of Casslynn in their bed, holding a cutter and telling him to spread his legs wide. She smiled at his hard on while weighing his balls in her delicate hand and ready to cut them.

Goodness! What is he thinking?

Chapter 2

"OH my, my Casslynn. Honey, this is perfect."

She met with her editor. She showed her the initial draft of her next book. And as she expected, her eyes are glowing with joy.

Yes, she's going to write on Andrew's book. Oh, she mean Alexis.

Speaking of that man, she saw his messages. But she didn't reply to any of it. She feels something for him. And she doesn't want to give in to this feeling because she could only get hurt in the end.

"Do you have any idea for the cover?"

She came back to her real world when her Editor, Emily, suddenly asked her about the book cover.

"I'm still thinking. Do you think my book will hit?"

Emily glared at her.

"Seriously? You're asking me that? Honey, did I hear some doubt in your voice? Most of your books are bestsellers' and this one is just going to be another."

She could not understand. But she had this feeling that she won't be able to finish this book.

"Not really, Em. But this one is going to be one hell of an erotic love story."

"Well, that is better. The more erotic it is the more people will love to read it." She read her draft again. "How did you come up with this idea by the way?"

Before she decided to meet Emily she prayed that she won't ask, but now she just asked it and lying to her means she can't sleep well.

"Ahm, it's an inspiration by a friend." It's half-true.

"Male friend?" She questioned suspiciously.

"Do you really need to know, Em?"

"Of course, honey. Now tell me about him."

It wasn't a request. Her life is Emily's business as much as she wants to deal with her book.

"His name is Alexis. I'm using his real name in my book." And she began to recall how she met Alexis in FindSome.com and how they also shared photos in Netto.

"What a sexy legs. It makes my knees weak."

She log in to her FindSome account daily. Normally, the men she met online are all assholes and perverts. If they don't wish to see her vagina and breasts they would ask her to friend invite in Netto for on-cam sex. But today is different.

"I love your beautiful legs, *ganda*."

She got two messages from someone named "Andrew A." He is from the same country she lived.

"Hi. Really? How can you like my legs and not my face?" Well, it's not that she's very proud but she knows she's beautiful.

"You are beautiful, but your legs are even more beautiful. How old are you?" He asked.

"I'm 26 and single. How about you? What's your name?" The usual questions she asked whenever she chat with someone new.

"Andrew. I'm 39."

"Okay. So I see you're from my province. How long have you been in this country?"

"More than two years now." He asked.

"Oh. So how much do you know of our language?" He is handsome. He has beautiful, blue eyes. He must be of Irish decent.

"Verbally is about 60%, but my comprehension is pretty good. Most often than not, I speak of your language."

"Wow, that's impressive for someone who only lived here for more than two years. Are you married?"

"LOL. No."

"What's funny about being married?" She's upset by the way he answer.

"I'm not the marrying type." A straight forward answer.

"Okay. But do you have a girlfriend?"

He sent a smiley. Then a big, **"NO."**

"Really? So why are you in our country?"

"**Business.**"

"**Hmmm. What kind?**" She's thinking he might be selling drugs.

"**I know what you're thinking. I'm not selling drugs.**"

He may be smart. How he can he read her mind over the net?

"**I did not say that.**" She said. Sounded defensive.

"**Ha ha. Bar and restaurant.**" She felt so stupid. How can this man laugh at her? She didn't reply.

So he asked her the same question this time. "**So, are you married?**"

"**I'm not. That's why I'm here. I'm looking for someone to marry, give me kids, and love me.**"

"**You can't find him here. All men here are horny.**"

She sent a crying smiley.

He sent a hugging smiley.

"**So, you're saying I shouldn't be here?**" She asked.

"**Not really. But what I'm saying you stop believing that you'll find him here.**"

"**Okay. But I will still keep looking. Why are you not married at your age yet?**"

"**I simply don't want to get married.**"

"**Don't you like kids?**"

"**No, I don't. Though I have a child with my ex long ago. But I have not seen the kid and his mother for years now.**"

"**You're so bad. How can you disown your child?**"

"**I didn't disown him. It's just that I don't like his mother.**"

"**Why did you get her pregnant in the first place? Don't you love her?**"

"**I don't believe in love, *ganda*.**" He simply said. She feels like he's making a full stop there.

"**Why?**"

"**I just simply don't.**" She's speechless. "**Tell me about yourself.**"

She log out right away.

"Hmmm. So do you find him handsome?"

She could sense her face is growing red.

"Hmmm?" She asked again still reading her draft.

One thing she learned in her 6 years of working with Emily is not to make her asked the same question thrice. She will be furious. Yes, that's Emily Higgins.

"Well, yes. But not really my type. It's just that I got curious in his life story that I decided to write a book about him." Now that's what you call defensive.

"It was just a yes or no, honey. You don't need to be defensive." Now, Em, is looking at her full of suspicions.

"I know you, Em." Em is not just an editor, she's like her mother, too and she's the nosy type of a mother.

"Honey, what's wrong with looking for a man? C'mon, you're 26. It's been almost 3 years, move on."

Em knows her story. Her biggest failure.

"Alexis is not the man I am looking for."

"How did you know?"

"I don't even know him personally."

"Well, why don't you meet him? I'm sure he will get to his knees knowing that he is meeting the most famous and successful novelist in this country."

"Em, please."

"Okay, okay. But don't close your door, honey." She still insists.

She just laugh at her. Sometimes she wonders what made her work with Em this long. Saying no to her is like violating the President's law.

But not Alexis. He's not for her. She won't waste her time on him. She needs someone who can give her the happy family she wants, the loving husband and kids she dream.

"You're a bit pushy, Em."

"It doesn't matter. I need this book for the anniversary special." She firmly said.

That made her eyes widened with shock.

"You're kidding me, Em! I can write another book. Not this one, please."

Lucky Alexis if this book got featured in the anniversary special. But she'll be doomed. Anniversary special includes book signing with fans. Yes, she write well but she is not good at receiving compliments and most likely she'll be hiding from fans. This is what scared her. Her last book signing didn't turn out well. It broke her heart. That was three years ago and the pain is still there, seems real, breaking her apart.

Today, is a different thing. Knowing, Em, she will surely invite Alexis and it's a bad thing.

God! Not again.

Chapter 3

'**S**HE woke up feeling drowsy. She had been sleeping for hours. Where's Alexis? He could not be leaving her.' Panic started to run down her veins. Then....

Arg!

She throw her pillow on the wall. Feeling upset.

She's been at this chapter since last night. Why can't she finish this part? She's been writing for more than 10 years now for two publishing companies yet she's having hard time putting the right words together for this chapter, when Alexis left his girlfriend.

"Have you forgotten me, Master *ganda*?"

A message pop up in her computer screen.

Oh my goodness!

She forgot to go offline or at least invisible. Now Alexis is chatting her. Now, she's starting to panic. She's not really good at lying even when it's just chat.

"Ahm, hi, Alexis." She doesn't know what to say.

"Hiya, *ganda*."

"How are you?" Now, this is the line she's very good at.

"I'm good. My balls are aching for you, master. Where have you been?" Now, that's something she wasn't prepared to answer.

"A bit busy. You know, I have started to write on your book. How's the business?" She answered, ignoring his other message.

"Going good so far. I am glad you started on it. But don't you get some off?"

"I do. But I'm not really the outdoor type." It's true. She's mostly a home buddy. When you are living alone, it's either you'll go for adventure or the opposite and she's the latter.

"I have ideas for you but you wouldn't like my ideas." Then he sent two laughing emoticons, one in love and another wink emoticon.

"Hmmm what is it?"

"I won't tell you, you would say no, I know for sure."

She got curious and laugh at the way he conclude her firm answer of 'no'. **"Let me hear it. Beach? Ha ha".**

"Has to do with slapping and kicking my testicles."

Bummer! This man is filthy.

"Lol kidding, but yeah you should go to beach. Or maybe some other fun sight."

"Silly." All she could say. **"But yeah beach would be fun."** She then added.

"I really wish you would... then, maybe they stop being full for a while."

Oh, this man really want to be castrated. As he told her before, it's his biggest dream to meet the woman who will castrate him, make him surrender and stop his womanizing skills.

"You're crazy." She's running out of words.

"Maybe, but that's what I wanted you to do for me. Oh, I forgot, are you near to Andromeda or Tantalus?" He is talking about their residences.

"No. I'm far from these places. I live in Python town. But my office is located in Cassiopeia. I have been to Andromeda and Tantalus though. Lovely beaches."

"Oh, I see."

"So, have you been to any places in the north?"

"No, not yet, just as far as Cassiopeia."

"Hmm, okay. So what are your plans for the day?"

"Dunno yet. Full balls as always so I'm sure naughty stuff."

Here they go again. Back to his balls. And she pretty knows well she'll end up admiring his beautiful manhood again. Just like the first time Alexis showed him a photo of his naked male member it was stuck there in her mind, like a bomb and ready to trigger the detonator. Unluckily,

Alexis himself is the detonator. She should not meet him. She is no longer the innocent type. She had sex few times with his ex, but she never admired his ex's penis the way he adored Alexis'.

"Sucks." He continued.

"How do you find pleasure in that? I mean, do you really enjoy it?"

"Yes I do. It feels good to get my sperm out of my testicles. But honestly wanting to have my testicles removed."

"Ha ha. Why don't you find a wife?" It sounded like a joke but she was serious.

"No kidding. I find it very sexy to think of... a woman cutting them off. Feeling submitted by her."

"I'm sure you have met qualified women to be your wife. In that way you don't have to do it alone." She insists in having him answer her previous question.

"Not really no, plus not sure I want to ever marry."

She just send him a laughing emoticon.

"I know it sounds weird to you but I desire it... to have a sexy woman castrate me. Thinking of her every time I look down and see them missing."

Now because he insists in getting castrated she will give in to his idea.

"If I would do that, trust me, you won't reach your 40th birthday."

"Why? If you would castrate me I would love it... I would be submitted to you and forever think of you. Winding if you keep them or toss them away after."

"I don't think a man will ever live after cutting his balls."

"True. It submits me as I no longer desire to breed."

"OMG!" That surprised her. "Really? You don't want kids?"

"Nah. If you wanted the sperm before cutting them off you could have."

"That's so sad. You're handsome." She felt really sad for Alexis. She admire his handsome face so much and she would want to ask him about his kid with his ex as she remembered he told her once, but thinking it isn't the right time.

"Grrr I'm so erect talking to you about this... so want it done." He seemed ignoring her sympathetic message. She also ignored his.

"Mind telling me why you don't want a kid?"

"Funny you never thought of doing that to a man before though, seems like most girls do think about it." She still doesn't like his response. But then he is still typing. "I don't mind having if the woman wanted one, but it would be up to her."

"Hmmm."

"Tell me what you're thinking *ganda*."

"Well, before, to me having a kid is a very big responsibility. I wasn't ready. But now I am." She honestly told him.

"Yeah, you would make a good mommy."

"But I have a big problem."

"**What?**" He sent an emoticon raising eyebrows along with this question.

"**I'm also scared having a baby alone.**"

"**Yeah it's a scary thing but if it happened you would do great. Hopefully you meet a guy to marry soon. If you don't then I don't know what to say.**" Sent along with this message is a sad emoticon.

"**Yeah, I'm praying for that.**"

"**I'm sure it will happen.**"

"**So, what did you have for breakfast today?**" She changed the topic. She still had not eaten so she's trying to get an idea from him of what to eat this morning.

"**I have not eaten yet, not hungry.**"

"**Oh, me, too.**"

"**I did something else... was messy.**"

"**Haha. You know what, I'm wondering how many women you slept with.**"

"**A lot.**"

"**So, how many did you get pregnant?**"

"**I got one baby but the woman was super abusive and dangerous so I left her.**"

"**Oh you got a baby.**" Now is the right time to ask him.

Blank. No reply from him. She waited few seconds. One minute passed. Five minutes. Ten minutes. Poof. He was offline.

She got curious. He had a kid. But he said he doesn't want to have one.

I think I know what to write now.

She smiled.

Chapter 4

H E went out of the country for two weeks. He didn't contact Casslynn all those days that he was out. It surprised him that she was the first person who came into his mind the moment he step his feet in the airport.

He reached his room and opened his iPad. He will message her and see if she would reply. He knows he owe her an explanation about hanging up last time without telling her. And he told her about her son.

Ugh.

Second to his family, Casslynn is going to be the next person he will tell the story of his past.

But who's giving a shit? Casslynn is not really his woman so what is he afraid of.

She is just Casslynn. And that's all he knows about her.

His deep thought was interrupted by a message.

"Hey, handsome. Where have you been?"

"Hello, *ganda*. I just came back. Was out of the country."

"Thought you relocated to Mars."

"LOL." This is what he missed. Casslynn's simple jokes really made him laugh.

"Remember anything?" She asked.

This is what he expected. He knows Casslynn will not drop the subject about his 'kid'.

"I know I owe you an explanation."

"Hmmm... Start the explaining now." She demanded. No woman would ask him this way but her.

"Where do you want me to start?"

"Ahm, your baby?"

Ugh. Why this woman can just simply forget about what he said last time?

"Alexis?"

Okay, okay. He really can't stop her from asking.

"Yeah, just like what I told you, I got one baby. A boy. I wanted to be there for my baby but she would not let me unless I stayed with her and I didn't want to, she was really bad, pulling knives, hitting, and breaking my things."

She did not reply.

So he continued.

"I went to see her and my baby the last time and she started hitting me while I held him...that's when I decided enough, too dangerous for him."

"Ahh it was better you left her. I can't imagine a big guy like you is capable of getting abused." She sounded amused.

He sent a laughing emoticon.

"Good thing she didn't demand marriage. If that would be me, marry me or lose your balls." She joked. And that made him laugh.

"I would gladly surrender my testicles to you. I don't think you would cut them though." He ignored her question about not marrying his ex. He is not ready to tell her that part of his life yet.

Not yet? So you really plan to tell her in the future?

His other brain side is asking him again.

Grrr.

He just ignored it.

"No... I think I'd rather cut that thing there that's giving you erection...If you don't marry me."

Oh that was a threat. He loves thinking she would really do it.

"Would you keep it after?"

"No...I'm throwing it to the dogs." Then she sent a laughing smiley.

"LOL. But yeah if you cut my balls off then my dick don't get erect."

"After all, I don't want any other woman to see or touch it anyway. So, I will cut both."

Gross. She can't do it. Not his big gun.

But he didn't ask her.

"Mine is big, you would enjoy."

She came blank for a minute.

He knows Casslynn is not like the women he met. She's a bit conservative and might be shocked with the kind of topic they have.

She responded differently.

"I'm the jealous type."

"I really do like the idea of losing my testicles to you."

"I'm the faithful type... I'll chop them into pieces, put some seasoning and...."

"Honest, I wish you would."

If he met Casslynn in his early years in life he might have taken her seriously...and marry her, probably.

"...throw them to the dogs." He bet she laugh when she said it.

"That would be so sexy if you ate them."

"But just kidding. I can't even kill a cockroach..." He just laughed secretely. **"Yuck."** She may have realized the last thing he typed.

"Lol, see? I know you would not cut my balls."

"Well, even in my imagination I can't. I don't think someone who can cut balls is a human at all... Silly... I'm having creeps."

"Lol. Wrong. It makes her in control of him."

"And I don't think you are a normal human wishing to have your balls cut."

"Funny it gives you the creeps and not a little sexy feeling thinking of taking mine."

"You're crazy."

He knows Casslynn would really disagree to his idea. But he is tired of this life. Getting full balls every day is a punishment to him. He want to put an end to this suffering. And he is only thinking of Casslynn to castrate him and not any woman.

"**Seeing me lay there with legs spread as you reach down, look me in the eyes and slice.**"

"**OMG. I'm not a criminal. You're crazy. Ha ha.**"

"**Lol, it's not criminal if consent... I think you kind of like the idea.**"

"**Goodness! Do you think if I'd be that woman, I would feel complete as a woman without your balls? Omg.**"

"**A shame you don't want to see them, you might enjoy.**"

"**No...I might enjoy watching it in full though.**"

"**Yes, I could still get hard with pills. And would not stray on you.**"

No reply from her for a minute.

Then she started typing.

"**Crazy. Now you are slowly opening the door to temptation.**"

He get it. She just love watching his male member. Casslynn is really an amazing woman. She was honest when she told him she's no longer a virgin. And he's glad she only slept with one man. Something he doesn't understand why.

"**You could watch mine any time *ganda*.**"

"**Omg. Alexis, please don't tempt me.**"

Even the way she said her name is sexy.

Fuck!

He's aroused. Yet, this is only chat.

He wonder how much more Casslynn can do when he met her in person.

"Okay... I'm just going to sit here and think of you taking mine.""

"How can you give me handsome and pretty kids if you'd want me to cut your balls? Silly."

"I would give you a baby first and after you cut them off." It's making him excited to give her a baby. He bet the baby would be very pretty. Casslynn has this kind of face you would never get tired to stare at. **"To ensure I don't make more with others and stay submitted to you."**

"I want BABIES though."

"You can have more than one. But once you finish, you cut the balls to ensure no other woman gets some."

"Haha. You're amazing. This is the funniest moment I've ever had in FindSome." Then she sent an emoticon that's laughing and rolling its butt on the floor.

"I think you like the idea *ganda*. I know you do."

"Of having your babies... absolutely!"

"Well, I told you before I would father a child with you should you not find a husband. You deserve a cute baby and ours would be so cute."

He could not imagine Casslynn marrying another man but him. But it's a stupid idea.

She's been typing for almost a minute now. Her reply must be a paragraph.

"Hmmm... I might just consider that idea." He was wrong. She must have deleted what she's supposed to reply.

"It would be an honor."

"Opps not the cutting of your balls... Creepy."

"If you didn't want to, that's okay." He is thinking of giving her not just one baby. "But I think you like the idea." He foolishly insist his idea of castration again.

Which she only ignores.

"Will you, you know, do the thing? Or have it inseminated? So I can prepare. Haha."

"I would leave it up to you actually how...If you prefer sure I can come over and just play with mine until my sperm comes out and then you put in or I would prefer sliding my big one in you and naturally releasing inside you."

"Gosh that's hard... I mean, ha ha. I'm having a not so good imagination."

Now he is really getting a big hard on.

"Tell me... Of feeling my warm seed burst deep inside you?"

It took her another minute to reply.

"Do you think I won't die? I mean my ex was big, too, well to me IT was big enough, and you're even bigger... will I not die?"

Whew! A very innocent question.

"No. I would just went slowly for you dear. But yes, it gets big."

He go to the bathroom. Took a photo of his male member. Now in full hard on. And sent it to her.

"OMG! Really? You're not shy to show it to me?"

"No. I think if we would make a baby I should not be shy to you."

"Good gracious!"

"Bad size? Or too big?"

"It's huge. No, enormous. This was even bigger than the last time I saw IT."

"I'm in full hard on now, baby."

"Gosh."

"Lol. I imagine how you look. Hard to see my testicles in that picture but they big also, would release lots of sperm for you."

Again, she didn't reply for a minute.

"I bet they're enormous, too. Why would a woman leave a man with such beautiful God-given gift? Your wife will be the luckiest woman on earth." Then she sent a blushing emoticon.

"Some women don't like them big."

"Well, it's beautiful. Very beautiful."

He felt his face going red. Casslynn is amazing.

"I do like you that you find my male member beautiful, that's really sexy to hear actually."

"First time I've seen such enormous beautiful thing. I don't think I can ever get sleep tonight. Good gracious! 'He' is very beautiful, Alexis."

"Honestly I love that you enjoy the view of my member. Well, like I said if you don't end up married I will use him on you to make a beautiful-mixed baby."

"Silly... I'm having a wild imagination. Sorry I don't mean to fantasize it, I don't own you."

"Did you take a second look at him?"

"Second look? Are you kidding me? I can't take my eyes off it."

"I love the way you think of it."

"But you are beautiful.'

"Make me feel special down there. I've been told it's huge before but you say it so sexy calling it beautiful. May I know what's your favorite about it?"

"Well, goodness, I like everything about it."

"Good, I feel admired down there. Lol sexy feeling."

It's true. He looked at his face in the mirror and he's blushing! Casslynn is the only woman who told her that his manhood is beautiful.

"You're shaved...amazing... It has a nice beautiful shape, you have nice legs, clean groin. It's just perfect and beautiful."

"Thank you. Yes, I shave. If we were to make our child I would ask you shave also. So I could see and taste your cute feminine flower."

"I always shave. I don't like hair all over. Itchy."

"Good. Same."

Then she asked him the question he never expected.

"How can you easily share it to me? Do you share it to every woman you met here in FindSome?"

"Lol. No, honestly only one woman here had it but I do wish to have a baby and I like the woman you are, the way you are and how hard you work. I know my child would be safe in your care and I hope you would allow me to visit often to help out."

That is true. He just found out all of a sudden how he wanted to have another baby.

But this is a bad idea. Not again.

No, he will not going to have it with Casslynn. She is just a chat mate and that is all.

She went offline.

What happen back there?

He left confused. He is not falling for Casslynn. Not her. He will just hurt her in the end. Or she will, just like *her*.

Shit! He doesn't want to remember the past. He moved on. But did he really?

Chapter 5

"ARE you okay?

It was Shane. Shane is another writer under Em's care.

"Why? How do I look?" She asked her.

"Oh my Casslynn. You look like a ghost. Not having slept for hundred years." She handed her a mirror.

True. She has eye bugs and her face look very sleepy.

"It's nothing."

"What's nothing? Can't you see yourself in the mirror girl?" Shane is giving her the glaring look.

"I tried to finish few chapters. And you know me." That was only partly true. She finished about three chapters only because the rest of her evening was spent re-reading the FindSome conversation she had with Alexis yesterday.

That jerk! As always.

"This whole idea of having your book featured in the anniversary special is not doing you anything good. Maybe you should talk to Em about it."

"What are we going to talk about, honey?"

Em is in good mood today. Otherwise, she would be calling her name.

"Oh, hi, Em." She gave her a hug.

She is not supposed to be in the office today. But she felt like talking to her colleagues. Everyone is rushing their projects. It's almost end of the month and new titles will be released this month. As always Emily Higgins' team is on the top. Why not? She has Shane, Victoria and her in her team. All three of them are considered the bestselling authors of the present day. One thing she will never get used to. Among the three of them it's only her who is using a pen name. Both Shane and Victoria are using their real first names as author names. And in every book signing she's the only one missing. One agreement she had with Em not to show up except during Anniversary special which will be in two months and she felt like dying.

"So, is there something we need to discuss beautiful lady?" She asked her.

"Nothing really, Em." She has no plan to get into details of telling them about Alexis. Only Em knows why she created such story.

"Well, just look at her, momma and you'll see what you need to discuss about." Shane interrupted again. She gave her a killer look. Which made Shane stand and left her alone with Em. She has this look that her co-writers are scared of. She's the type who rarely smiles. Men easily fall for her when she smiles and that's the last thing she want to happen.

"So... what's with your look? Didn't you get much sleep?" Em asked her suspiciously.

"I tried to finish some chapters."

"Mmmm.. And what else did you do?"

"Em, please."

"Alright, young lady." Em gave up. "Now, follow us in the conference room."

Em rarely calls for a meeting.

"What for?"

"It's something about our team outing."

"I'm busy, Em."

"No excuses this time, Casslynn."

That's it. Em calls her Casslynn, when she do it, she mean seriously dead about something. So she has no choice but to join this outing.

Not again.

The last time she joined this outing she ended up dating a pervert guy. And few calls from other men after.

But then she really has no choice.

She followed everyone to the conference room.

And there everyone is looking like they're waiting for the arrival of the CEO.

"There she is." That was Victoria.

She gave her a warning look.

Victoria is the type who wants to do the first thing that came to her mind. Like if she wants her to date someone she will really do it. Or if she wants to tease her in the middle of a meeting she'll do it.

"I guess, Casslynn, has a great idea, Em. What do you think ladies? This young lass I bet is excited." It's Victoria again.

Yes, she is the youngest in Em's team. Shane is 40. Victoria is 36 and the rest of the 6 writers in this team are all in their late 30's. All are married but her.

"Not me, Victoria." She grimaced.

"C'mon Cass. When was the last time you came with us? Six months ago?" Said Carly, another writer.

They are trying to decide on which place to spend their team outing.

She tried to seek help from Em for her to stop these ladies from buying her out and join. But seems that Em is busy with her cellphone.

And Shane is just giving her a "decide now" look.

Victoria seems to enjoy.

"I will contribute 2K. I'm kinda busy so-"

"We have team funds, Cass." That was Drei, a mother of two.

Victoria is amused.

"Fine. There's a good place I know in the north."

"Not north, please. We were there last month." Shane protested.

"Well, I don't see the point why you ladies asked me!" She's pissed off now.

"We didn't." Everyone chorused, even Em.

"Okay, help me understand." She said slowly before she could shout at them.

"We asked you to come with us not give us the suggestion for a venue." It was Victoria.

"I can't."

"Why not?" Shane asked.

Why Em is not talking? She used to save her every time she's at the point of having no choice.

But Em just gave a shrug.

"I have stuff to do."

"Like what? Movies, reading books, online games, and alone?" Its Victoria again, sounded so annoyed now.

Everyone in her team knows she's single.

"You are wasting your beauty, dear. If I was that beautiful when I was 26, God knows how many boyfriends I have had." Freda said.

"Unfortunately, I agree with Freda." That was Adelaide. Freda and Adelaide don't go along together. They always fight on something. Another reason why she doesn't want to join this group in an outing since the two will only argue the whole time. But when it comes to her, they always agree on something to aggravate her.

"Alright. I will come. But promise me. Don't ever hook me with a guy again. Or I swear to heaven I am not gonna talk to all of you again. Right, Victoria?" It's always Victoria who do the naughty stuff. She's married to an American ten years her senior.

Victoria just gave her a wink.

"That's settled then." Said Em.

"And I know you would like my idea ladies." Shane said. "There's a good place in the south. One of my husband's friends invited us there once and the place is perfect."

"Okay. So...?" Jenna asked without glancing from reading her favorite fashion magazine.

"It's a beach. The only difference is that the owners do have bar and restaurant, too. Take note it's just inside the resort. And the owners are incredibly handsome." Shane continued, feeling excited.

"Help me remind you that you're married with three kids, Shane." She said, interrupting her excitement.

"No way, young lady. I'm faithful to my husband. In fact, one of the owners, Robert, is married to a Filipina. And he is the faithful type. Lucky, Rowena. But of course, I'm luckier to have Josef." Shane is also married to a foreigner, German she guessed.

She just gave a loud sigh.

She will never win against the desires of these women.

"We can bring our husband and kids I guess." Drei suggested.

"Of course. They have pool for kids. Gazebo, too. Sauna, Spas and all of that."

"And you said the owner of this resort are foreigners and single?" Victoria asked but it sounded like a statement while looking at her.

"Oh, please Victoria." She begged now. But Victoria just gave her a victorious smile.

"Not all of them. There were five. Only Rob is married. But yes, they are foreigners and handsome."

"But old people." As usual she's a spoiler.

Shane laugh.

"Rob is the oldest and he's 42. The rest are in their 30s. Well, if you call that old, Cass, suit yourself." Shane just winked.

"Do you have any estimated amount of total costs of our expenses?" Their accountant, Brenn, talked. She's the silent type, too, like her, but Brenn is married with one kid and she's not.

"Don't worry, not that expensive. I will call Rob later for arrangement.

"So, where is this place?" Asked Em, she look excited.

She may be the only person in this group who's not excited about this outing.

"Andromeda."

"No! Not there!" She said with a strong protest.

"Why?" Everyone chorused again, looked at her with questions.

"I mean, why there? There are other places. Tantalus maybe. Or we could go with some hotel in the city."

Andromeda is where Alexis lived. And who knows their paths might cross. No! She cannot meet Alexis. She cannot meet the detonator of her secret evil physical desire inside. Whenever she thinks of Alexis she has this feeling of having a fever, it's boiling inside her and the only remedy is not to think of his face which is working because she has some kind of unusual unfortunate ability of forgetting faces, but not the looks of his perfectly, beautiful male member. And right now, thinking of 'him', just made her wet.

"It's settled. Andromeda then." Em finally decided. "Shane, make the arrangement and you bring Brenn with you."

Seems like she was awakened from a deep, horny dream. "Em, please." She begged again. She really feel wet, still the clear sight of Alexis' big gun is distracting her.

"Honey, I don't see any reason not to stay in Andromeda. Also, it's good that Shane knows someone from that resort. Don't worry, you just need to bring yourself and get some swim. Okay?" She felt nervous and silently prayed she won't see Alexis. Well, she hoped too that she will forget his face, too.

Chapter 6

"WHAT are you doing?"

He almost fell from his seat.

"Hey, Rob." The only thing he said.

"You're working like hell bro. Are you trying to run away from something? Ben said you never take a day off."

"Of course not." He lied.

It's been almost a week since he last spoke to Casslynn. Which is a good thing. He got the chance to make up his mind. She kept telling him she wanted a kid and that she would make him the father of her baby. One thing he didn't want. He didn't want her to expect that he can fulfill her dream. A girlfriend is a big responsibility that's why he doesn't have one. A kid is even a greater responsibility and he didn't wish of having another responsibility other than his resort business.

"Then you might want to tell me why you're working like the world is going to end soon." Rob muttered.

"That's a crazy question, Rob. This is our business and I am taking this seriously." He reasoned.

"I know that. But bro, you're not getting a life."

"This is my life, bro."

"C'mon, Alexis. This is not you, bro. Are you going through some kind of love life issue?"

Rob know him very well. He is not really the workaholic type. He usually go out with girls. But here he is working like he fathered twelve kids.

He look around. No one seem to hear Rob.

"Help me remind you not to call me with that name in public."

"Tsk, tsk. I know you won't say a thing. But just remember that I'm the right person you can talk to if it's about your love life."

"Just go and do your job, Rob. And leave me alone."

"Alright, big boy. Just don't kill yourself."

Rob left him alone.

He gave a loud sigh.

Sometimes he hate being alone. Especially in times like this. His last conversation with Casslynn keeps coming back.

"Are you sure you don't want to get married?"

"No, *ganda*... there's no chance."

"Why, because you're afraid that you will marry someone like your ex?"

"Not really." He lied.

"That's sad. Not all women are like your ex. I would love to think of you as the father of my

children but I want a complete happy family that's why I want marriage. Marriage isn't easy as it is a lifetime commitment. A promise that you'll love your spouse no matter what, stay by his side when he gets old and ugly whether he's still has money or not. This is something I am looking for in a man and this can only happen in a relationship with God's blessing and that's marriage."

"I agree. You're right. Honestly, I don't think you will need my sperm, I think the right man will come into your life soon. But if for some reason years down the road it doesn't happen then my balls are yours to use."

Then he ended up saying goodnight to her.

But he really didn't have a good night.

All those things she said really hit him deep. He didn't even get the interest to get some sex. He just bore himself to death by working so hard.

But he's still waiting for her to go online and send her a message. She never did. Now he is feeling empty.

Chapter 7

THIS month is the busiest month of the year. Anniversary will be in one month's time and everyone is occupied preparing for the big event.

She didn't hear from Shane and Victoria or even from Em. She's almost finish with Alexis' book.

Today, she's too lazy to do anything.

She wants to message Alexis, but she knows if she did, they will both have that horny moment and will end up just having on cam sex. Alexis is wild on cam. She can't imagine how wilder he would be in person. No doubt girls will cling into him. He is adorable. Plus handsome and smart. On top of it all, his intelligence is what she admired the most. Every person who knows her said no one can match her intelligence but they didn't meet Alexis yet. How she wish they meet in a different time and situation. Maybe, just maybe, there will be a chance for them.

She just re-read their previous conversation, some of them made her smile and cry, but this one they had few weeks ago really made her wet.

"Are you still looking at my male member?" She remember she blushed when he asked her this and now she blushed again.

"Sort of. But please don't tempt me again."

"Well, if you ever feel like being tempted I can show you more in Netto."

They were chatting in FindSome at that time.

"Well why not."

"I would enjoy showing you the testicles I want you to step on or kick and squeeze."

"I want to keep the photo you had, when you were in full hard on. I love that one."

"I am fully hard right now. I actually sent you a video in Netto for you to watch."

"Hmmm. Wow. Thank you. Let me see."

She remembered she went to see his video and she was surprised.

"Omg! Oh your big gun. It's so pink and big. And so does your balls. You are really gifted."

"Yes. But I want the balls cut."

"I can't. They're too beautiful to get bruised. Of course, the big gun is even more beautiful."

"I sent another."

She came to look for another video. It showed his balls tied in thread.

"Oh gosh, remove the thread, your balls are hurting, please."

"Can't I keep them tied as we chat? I like feeling them sore for you since I admitted my deepest desire to you."

"You're crazy. Remove the thread, have mercy on your balls."

"I'll leave the choice up to you *ganda*."

Then he sent another message after few seconds.

"But someday I would love to see your little sexy feet...for me it's the biggest turn on a woman's feet... seeing them in the air from the bottom side as I would seem them while inside her."

"Really? Leg is your weakness?"

"Feet, yes."

"Ohh, that's something new to me. Why? What's with the feet?"

"I enjoy kissing or sucking them. Or having my balls stepped on or kicked... I know... odd."

She really do have beautiful legs and clean feet.

"Wow, really? You're weird."

"Only tried that once but I liked it."

"Hmm, I have never suck a penis. I didn't do it with my ex."

"Wow. I love to be your first then. And if you decide to castrate me who knows, maybe I stay as your submissive male."

"Castrating you feels like I'm a criminal, I can't do it."

"You like the idea a little though I bet."

"Honestly, I'm having second thoughts."

"About?"

"About castrating you."

"Good. I hope you would. It's a very personal offer. You would have power over me being the woman to remove those testicles. Looking at me as those big warm balls lay in your hand after. And anytime I look down at my missing balls I would think of you and that night."

"This is hard. I'm trying to absorb everything I learned from today. I can't get over with your beautiful manhood. It's just perfect, so perfect."

"I love that you admire him."

"But sorry, I can't show you anything in return." Of course she can't let him see her breasts or vagina. That's another thing.

"I know you won't show me your feminine flower. But I love to see those feet. Someday maybe you show me a picture of them."

"Who knows one day it might not be photo but the real one."

Creepy. Why in the world did she say that?

"If it do means you didn't find the one and although the male side of me wants to enjoy every inch... I know it's better if you find your man to marry."

That was the last thing he bid before he said goodnight.

She scroll down and read other conversation from a different date.

"My goodness, Alexis, you just uploaded something. Please remove the photo I don't want anyone to see it."

"Oh, sorry, *ganda*, didn't mean it. This app is really a mess. That's why my photos were only set to friends only."

She sent an angry emoticon as a response to that. Then she yelled at him.

"Oh, you're other friends can see it, too. Remove it. Now!"

"Only I have one friend here."

She remembered how relieved she was knowing that she is the only friend of Alexis in FindSome. And she felt a little pride.

After going through each messages which are all filthy things coming from Alexis, she turned off her laptop.

Then her eyes move towards the calendar.

She has less than two months to prepare for the outing. She is dying to ask Alexis where in Andromeda he lives. But then knowing Alexis he would surely ask why. She can't tell him she's coming to Andromeda. She can't meet him. She prayed she would get very sick on that day and she needs to be admitted to the hospital. That's the only thing that could save her from going to the outing.

Yes, she's afraid to meet him. Because now she's falling for him and meeting him in person will worsen the situation.

How she wish her parents and sister are alive. Maybe she will not get herself into this kind of sadness and longing to be part of someone's life. Someone like Alexis.

Chapter 8

"AHHH, faster..."

He's in the hotel with this petite woman named Natalie. Or he's not even sure if that was her name.

He is having a good sex with this woman. Though he is thinking of Casslynn.

SHIT!

Casslynn again. That woman is a witch. She never go off his mind. He has not message her for almost a month now. He had fuck almost ten women since then yet he's still thinking of Casslynn.

"Fuck, Andrew! I said faster. Why did you stop?"

"Get off me." She's on top of him. He said coldly.

"What? Why?!" She now looks like a tigress.

"I will send you home, Natalie."

"Bullshit! My name is Yanni."

"Whatever."

He push her and went to the rest room.

"When I finish my shower, I want you gone. Give me your account number if you need money." That's all he said and left her.

Inside the shower room, he's seeing Casslynn naked and smiling at him.

Shit! He almost went soft earlier, and now after seeing Casslynn's smile he's back to full arousal again.

Damn! Damn! What's with you, Casslynn?

I think he should meet her and fuck her so hard. He would raise her lovely legs in the air while sipping her and make sure her eyes will glow with orgasm. He would suck her nipples so hard until she scream his name.

Shit! He had been fucking women yet he still not had enough.

I need to see my friends. I need to go back burying myself to work.

He turn off the shower. Just then he heard his phone ringing.

It was Ben.

"Yo."

"Where are you? No one's answering your home phone. Buddy, Rob is mad."

If Rob is the Daddy type, Ben is the big brother type. Ben has a girlfriend and they are planning to get married this year.

Sucks! Another stupid man. He called them stupid those who want to settle down. Being single is fun. Less responsibility, less worry.

"I'm in the hotel. But about to check out."

"Oh gross. Another victim of your charm tonight."

"Mind your own business, Ben." He is now fully clothed. "So what's the story?"

"We have clients. They're from LGP, I guess."

"What's that?"

"It's a publishing company. I forgot what it means. But get your ass over here or Rob will fetch you and punch you on the face, irresponsible lad."

"Not again, Ben. I'm on my way." Ben does have a future of becoming a pastor. He's good in lecturing him about what's right and wrong. Poor guy. He will soon be imprisoned forever with one of Eve's cursed sisters. He's talking about Maridelle, Ben's girlfriend.

He's driving his Nissan car. This is his all-season car where his women can get a ride. He also has this special car. His Lamborghini. He called it Medusa. No one rode that car but him. Not even his friends are allowed to ride with him when he's driving Medusa.

He reached the resort after 30 minutes. He met the ever grumpy Rob.

"What's up?" He greet him with smile.

"Where have you have been, asshole? Why the hell did you not answer your phone?" Rob didn't even smile a bit.

"I'm on my personal business, Rob. Thought you told me to get a life."

"You talk to him, Rob. I have nothing to do with reservations. I'm out here." Franky left, looking annoyed.

"I will go to the counter, Rob." Ben left without waiting for Rob's answer.

"I need to do some accounting of our emergency funds." Charlie heed for the elevator.

Rob angrily throw some papers on the table.

He saw that those are the lists of people or companies that made advance payment for reservations next month. He's the one handling the bookings and reservations for the resort.

"What's wrong with these? Are the charges wrong? I believe these are our normal rates for reservations." He's confused what made Rob so mad.

"Not the rates, idiot!!" He's cursing. No, Rob is not mad. He is furious.

"What then?"

"Didn't I place a special note on your computer, even sent you a message, even tell the other guys, NOT to make the private penthouse vacant?"

Holy shit!

He remembered now. That's what he missed. Rob did inform them a month ago that the private penthouse is reserved.

"Well, I guess I could just tell the teachers that the penthouse is taken." He got it reserved for teachers from a certain college.

"Not that easy. I spoke to the head teacher and they are not accepting reimbursement."

"I can fix this." He doubt if he can. But he will use his charm again. To hell if he needs to fuck those teachers. Don't care if they are old.

"Well, then, big guy, fix it if you can. But I need you to know that the private penthouse was reserved for friends from Love Grow Publishing."

"They're group of writers?" He wonder if Casslynn is one of them.

"They are not just writers, lad. They are group of successful writers from this country. When I say successful, the books they wrote usually go out of print in a matter of week. That's how good they are."

He doesn't have any idea how successful Casslynn is. But she said her books usually hit in the market.

"Oh, that's interesting. How old are these writers?"

"No man. You don't stand a chance. These writers though group of beautiful women are all married. HAPPILY married with KIDS." Rob said emphasizing the words 'happily' and 'kids'.

"Okay. How long is the penthouse reserved for them?"

"No limit. But they will be here in a month's time."

Chapter 9

"CONFIRMEDDD!"

That was Shane, shouting at the top of her lungs upon coming to the office.

"What's confirmed?" Drei asked.

Good thing Em isn't around or Shane will be kicked out of the office.

"We got the reservation from Pentagon Knights." She said excitedly.

"Oh, that's great." Drei simply said and went back to work.

"What's that? You ladies are going out again? Didn't your husbands complain that you're living like singles?" She asked without lifting her eyes from the computer.

"Seriously, Cass, you didn't know?"

"What should I know?"

"Oh my goodness, I can't believe you didn't read my email!" Shane sounded hurt.

"There's no importance notice. So I just archived it."

"I told you to add an importance mark or she will ignore it." That was Victoria. Just came in with her little girl. "Okay baby, go to the pantry and eat your cookies. I will have a little chit chat with Tita Cass before we watch Elsa, okay?"

"Yes, mommy." Said the little girl. "Hello, Tita Cass. You are so beautiful today."

"Oh wow, cutie. Thank you. Come, give me a kiss." Victoria's daughter gave her a quick kiss on the cheek before running to the pantry.

"Okay, so where we at?" Shane interrupted. "And that little girl is very lucky, she always got your smile." Her smile faded.

"See? I told you only little girls get her smile." She didn't know Drei stopped from her work just to make that comment.

"Why do you always have to make my smile a big thing?"

"Well, young lady, if you didn't know, when you smile you made everyone's knees weaken. Do you even have the slightest idea that when you smile you become even more beautiful?" Shane gave her a compliment which made her blush.

"With that smile, you could fool a thousand men, young lady." Drei added.

"Stop! Please." She always hear it from them, from anyone. She's beautiful, smart, sexy, etc. She sounded like a perfect creation of God but she's not. And to prove it, she's not happy.

Drei just smirked and went back to her work.

"Okay. So, anyone wants to explain to me about this Pentagon Knights?" She changed the topic.

"Oh my goodness!" Drei, Shane, and Victoria glance at her altogether, with unbelievable looks.

"I have no idea." She honestly said.

"Okay. I guess I should tell you. Oh, why do I have to explain things to you, Casslynn, you of all people!" Shane rolled her yes. "Anyway, for your information, and make sure you remember this because not only that you are forgetful of people's faces, their names, too."

"Whatever. Just go directly to the point." This time she made rolling eyes.

"Pentagon Knights, young lady, is where we have our reservation for the team outing in Andromeda. The resort is owned by five handsome men that they call themselves knights."

She went silent. But then was able to pick up herself after few seconds.

"I thought the outing was canceled." She really thought it was. Well, no one had talked about it since weeks or so ago.

"Why do I have this feeling that you're not coming, Casslynn?" Victoria said, sounded frustrated.

"I just-" She cut her off.

"And don't tell me you'll get sick on that day. Swear to heavens I'm gonna drag you to the car just to bring you to Pentagon Knights. And not until you got yourself tied in the hospital bed there is no other acceptable reason that you can make." She didn't yell at her yet but she knows that Victoria is mad. "And excuse myself, I will go to my daughter now and we will watch Frozen. If I have calls just send them to my voicemail." Then she walked out.

"Well, just great, you made her mad and I bet, this means whole day of us not being able to use the movie room." Drei pouted.

The last time Adelaide made Victoria mad, she stuck herself in the movie room for whole day.

"I have no plan to use the movie room anyway. But I want to agree with Victoria. Don't you ever try to make excuses young lady." Shane warned her before going inside her office. While Drei is facing her computer again.

She was left alone.

God!

She feel so scared of going to Andromeda. She has the feeling that she will going to see Alexis there. That feeling of boiling heat inside her. She felt her face getting red. Seeing him naked just made her excited.

Please go off me, devil!

She speak to the air silently.

Chapter 10

SHE heard them talking. Em, Shane, Victoria, Drei, and her other five co-writers. They're here. She's awake, yet she can't move. What's wrong with her?

Then she saw man and woman running in the seashore. The man was calling her "honey". The man looks hot. The woman is petite but she has a very beautiful smile. She's pretty. Just then she realize something. The guy, it's him! The asshole who broke her heart. And the woman he was running after, that's, that's... her.

Then the images fade, and memories came. All bad memories came back flashing like browsing history stored in Google Chrome. The only thing different is that she cannot erase them. One by one, each memory break in... she's back to where she was, the time when she thought she was the happiest woman on earth.

Someone or something covered her eyes. She knows these hands.

"Henry, honey, I know it's you." She said.

"I thought you would say someone else's name." Her boyfriend smiled. He's bringing a single rose flower. As always her boyfriend cannot afford to buy her a bouquet. She doesn't really like rose. Tulips is her favorite but it's a very expensive flower. But she doesn't care. She loves him. 'You're a fool! What in the world did you see in that man?' Her father used to yell at her. He felt a total disgust against Henry.

"Anything wrong, honey?" He asked. He's kind of dumb as well. Can't really guess if she's mad or sad. But she still loves him.

"I had a fight with, Dad, again." She's trying to make it sound normal but the truth is she wants to burst into tears. Her family...no...

Henry's face turned from excited to mad then to sad. She can easily read his emotions.

"I guess it's about me again."

"I'm sorry, honey." All she could say.

From sad he is now back to being mad. "What is it this time again? If not my job, my being uneducated, what else could your father said?"

"He thinks you're into drugs."

She thought she saw him turned pale. Was that guilt she saw in his face?

But he turned from mad to furious.

"Why on earth your father accused me of using drugs? I know he doesn't like me for you. He accused me of all bad things in the world but drugs? That's insane!"

"Is it true?" She just wanted to know. Yes, she accepted all his imperfections. Yes, he has a nice job but with low pay. He's handsome but he didn't finish college. That is okay. But if she found out her father's accusation is true. He can't forgive this man.

"Are you accusing me, too? Do you believe your father this time? He is trying to ruin our relationship. He is trying to make you break up with me. We are getting married and we should not be discussing this." She sensed him getting away from her question.

"You can simply answer my question with a yes or no, Henry. You don't have to talk too much." She's trying to stop herself from yelling at him.

Just then his phone rings.

He pull out the cellphone from his pocket and she saw it. He went pale after looking at his cellphone screen.

"Who is that?" She grab the phone from his hand without hesitation.

'CHELLE SWEET'

That's the name of the caller.

"Who is she?" She's trying to stop her voice from breaking. Trying to stop her tears. Her father must be right.

'That guy is fooling you. He's into drugs and you're stupid not to notice that. He also has another girlfriend other than you.' Her father told her before him, her mother and sister went away on a trip without her.

"Give me that, Casslynn! You should not grab my phone without my permission!"

But she didn't hand him the phone. She answered it without saying a word. A woman speak on the other line.

"*Sweet, where are you? Are you not done with Casslynn yet? Ask her the money now and get your ass back here. Your order just arrived.*"

"*This is Casslynn, Chelle. And I'm amazed that you know me at all. How long have you two fooled me? Well, congratulations, you made me look stupid, but no, you won't get any money from now on. And oh, the money that Henry gave you, I didn't give it, I lend it to him and you will pay it with interest.*"

Then she ended the call. Throw the phone into the sea.

"*Why the hell did you do that?*" *Henry glared at her. As if nothing happened. As if he didn't make any mistake. She had pre-marital sex with him thinking that he will be her husband, but she's been blinded.*

She gave him twin slap. She wanted to punch him but she is not that brutal.

"*It's over! I want you to get lost! Get lost for good. Because now, I hate you, Henry, I hate you so much! Nothing you can do to earn my forgiveness. It costs my family's life, this stupid love that I felt for you. I can never forgive you!*"

Then off she goes, to the funeral parlor, where the bodies of the three people she love are lying. Her father, mother, and sister. They're dead. And she was left alone, with no one, with nothing. And she's heart broken.

"I hate you, Henryyyyy!!!"

She shout to the deep of her lungs.

It feels like something or someone had pulled her out from a deep pit. From that dark place came a light. It's hurting her eyes.

"Goodness, Casslynn! You're awake!" That was Shane. She saw her crying. "Em, Victoria, Drei, Adelaide, Jenna, Brenn, Carly, Freda, come over! She's awake!"

All nine ladies came rushing to her.

"Oh my God, let me call the doctor." That was Victoria. She never seen her so panic before.

"Let me see if she's okay. Honey? Do you feel any pain? Which part is hurting?" Though she flooded her with questions, Em is crying, crying like she's going to die.

"Are you hungry, Cass?" That was Jenna. She barely speaks to her, but now she's worried like hell.

"You've been sleeping for three months now!" Yelled Shane, but she looks pretty worried.

"We thought you will never wake up." Drei said who is now trying to massage her arm.

"Goodness, Cass, just as you are a magnet to men so does to accident." Adelaide said whose eyebrows raise but she can't hide the worry in her eyes.

"What happen?" The only words she said.

Each of them is looking at one another trying to decide who will tell her the complete story.

"You had an accident. You left sad in the office that day, a week before we go off our outing. A bystander said you were running away, crying and trying to cross the street when you were hit by a fast running car. Good thing the driver brought you to the hospital right away. But you were comatose. And today, after three months of lying here, you wake up." It's Em who decided to speak. As usual their editor, their mother and supporter.

She tried to think what happen on that day.

Yes, she left the office, she's in a rush trying to get home to finish some chapters. She's writing her next book after Alexis'.

Alexis!

That name. She must have heard that somewhere. She's trying to think, but oh, her head just grow a different kind of pain, it's something unbearable.

"Are you okay? Casslynn!" Brenn shouted. "Dammit! Where's Victoria? What's taking her so long?"

"I'm okay. My head just hurts."

"That must be due to the accident. You hit your head pretty bad." Carly said.

"Who's Henry?" Freda wondered.

Em was looking at her suspiciously. Only Em knows her story before she officially joined the team three years ago. Em had been her personal trainer.

"He's someone from Casslynn's past. But we should not talk about him here, not now." Em is now acting like her mother. She's 52 anyway and maybe if her mother was alive Em could be a good bestfriend.

The doctor came in.

He asked her few questions which she was able to answer perfectly. She's the intelligent Casslynn, any type of question can be answered by her genius mind.

"You look pretty good. But we need you to undergo another brain scan, just to be sure."

The doctor tried to scribble something in his record, when he asked her something.

"Is there anything that bothers you, a name of place, maybe person or thing but you can't remember?"

Alexis!

Why that name rings a bell.

"I'm not sure, doctor, but there's a name. Alexis. I know this somewhere I guess. But my head hurts when I tried to remember where I've heard this name."

"Silly, that's the name of your lover boy in your book. Which unfortunately was released without you during the anniversary special." Shane sadly.

Em interrupted.

"What does that mean, doctor? She remembered us, she remembered everything in the past but Alexis."

The doctor mumbled. But no one bothered to ask.

"Hmmm... I don't understand, too. I'm sure you know this person. But I guess until you make personal contact with this person or maybe do the things you used to do before, you won't be able to remember the name. But we will do further study and let you know. For the meantime, the nurse will bring you to the other building for brain scan."

"We will wait for you outside, Cass."

Everyone rushes outside except Emily.

"So, is there something you need to tell me?" Emily asked when they were alone.

She began to burst in tears.

"Okay, honey, let it all flow." Em is trying to comfort her.

It took her forever to stop the tears but she was able to talk.

"I saw him with Chelle before the accident, Em. That bastard and that bitch are still together. My family's death is haunting me. That idiot was there even in my dreams, ah, nightmares I guess."

"Honey..." All Em can do is to cry, too.

"I thought I have moved on, Em. I thought I am a new person now. But I'm still the same person. The same weak woman. The broken-hearted. The lost." She's still crying.

"Do you want to go out of the country?" Em suggested.

"No. That will make me feel worse. Ah, do we still have that reservation in Pentagon Knights?" She remembered about the place that Shane reserved for their outing. She didn't know why she feel excited. Em look worried.

"Are you sure? You were hesitant to join in this outing before."

"Really? Why?" She's confused. Pentagon Knights seemed like a wonderful place.

"I should asked you the same question."

"Isn't it just a beach resort with bar and restaurant as Shane said before?" Feeling more confused. "Why would I hesitate to visit the place?"

"Honey, that puzzles me, too. But my guess-" She didn't finish her sentence. This time Em look amused.

"What?"

"I thought at first, it has something to do with Alexis. I thought he live in Andromeda and you're afraid to meet him there."

"That name again. Are you sure it's only a character name in my book?"

"Well, partly. But are you sure you can't remember him? He was your friend from FindSome, you wrote that book for him." Em confessed.

"Really? Wow, now I'm starting to believe I'm a good writer coz I can create a non-existing character. The name rings a bell, Em, but I can't even remember his face."

"You're not really good at remembering faces and names of people, Cass."

"But this one is worst, there's really no link I can connect to remember him." She sounded frustrated now.

"Hmmm, let's drop this subject then. Don't force yourself to remember the name, maybe he's not that important. The nurse is here."

Not important.

Not important.

Not important.

It echoed in her mind. But why on earth she remembered the name?

Chapter 11

Krrrrrnnnggggg!!!!

Shit!

That was his alarm.

Why the hell did it ring again?

He throw it away.

He heard a cracking noise. It's breaking into pieces.

Shit!

Then he heard a music, it's the song of Jesse McCartney, 'Leavin''. It ring so loud that he really can't go back to sleep now.

Now he's getting more annoyed, frustrated, angry... Ahh, it was his cellphone. He likes Jesse M's song so much that only his songs are saved in his music player.

When he saw whose calling.

It's Robert.

"Yo." He answered, sounded so sleepy.

"You're still sleeping? What time is it, Alexis Isaiah? It's almost lunch. Do you know that I had the other three called you but you didn't pick up your phone?"

Blah! Blah! Blah!

Dah! Dah! Dah!

He's trying to cover his ears.

If only Rob is not a friend and a business partner he could have yelled at him now. 'Go to hell, man, I don't need you!' But of course that's all in his mind, he can't say it loud to Rob.

"I sleep late last night. What's up?"

"It's the 28th of the month, Alexis!" He must be inside the bar because he could hear the music in the background, and he's just calling him his real name. Fuck Robert!

But he is still trying to respond nicely.

"So, what's with the date?" Still sounded so sleepy.

"Get your ass off here now, Alexis Isaiah or I'm gonna send a messenger to your condo now and plant a bomb! Our guests from LGP are coming!"

Shit! This group of writers again.

It reminded him of someone.

Casslynn.

It's been three months. Never heard a word from her. The last time he was logged in to Netto and FindSome was more than three months ago. Ah she must have found her man!

He's surprised to feel a little pain inside him. *Well, it's normal, you didn't get the chance to fuck her.* The other side of his brain reasoned. Casslynn is truly a goddess, the perfect woman for him. The legs, wow, lovely, and lips so perfect, he's sure can't get enough of her. And the body, shit, just perfect for his size. And the smile. Holy shit! He's aroused again just thinking of the way she smiled. He never had the chance of talking to her live on cam just sharing of photos, but he saw her smile and she's goddam pretty, a goddess, can't help him getting a hard on.

He got another call from Rob.

"I know you're still in bed. I am serious, Alexis, we need you here in the resort now or I will really send someone to cast a flea in your home."

That is a warning. He knows when Rob is mad and when he's joking.

He is still very hard just thinking of Casslynn's smile. He will release this disturbing sperm inside the bathroom.

How he wish he got the chance to get castrated by Casslynn before she can even meet her man.

Oh that pretty witch. Still her beauty is haunting him!

Would there be a chance to really meet Casslynn in person without a man with her? He only wants to be the only man in Casslynn's life.

So you will you marry her then? Give her a baby?

Said the other part of his brain.

Hell, no!

Chapter 12

"GIVE that to me!"

"No! This is mine. Mommy, can you tell Sab not to steal my hairbrush?"

"That's mine, Abby, you stole that from my bed last night!"

The pretty daughters of Victoria fighting over a pink hairbrush of Barbie. And there's Mon, Victoria's husband, trying to stop his daughters from fighting.

"C'mon, Abby, give the hairbrush to your little sister. I will buy you one when we get to the resort."

"But dad." She pouts. But handed out the brush to Sab.

They are traveling to Andromeda. Any minute from now they will arrive in Pentagon Knights.

Long ago, she dreamed of having kids her own, loving husband, happy family. But not anymore, maybe because of the accident. Of the bad memories that she tried to erase, they were all restored, changing her back to her old self. The old Casslynn who's scared, selfish, and uncertain. If there's one thing she didn't want this time, its responsibility, having a child is a problem. Keeping a husband is even a bigger problem. She has enough problems in her life.

"You look sad. What are you thinking?"

Holy cow! She almost fell from her seat. That was Em, trying to ask her something. She forgot that she's in a group of ladies inside this van. With her, other than Victoria and her family, are Shane with her kids and husband, Drei, Freda and Em.

"Nothing, Em." She lied. She's surprised how she can easily lie without feeling any guilt. One thing her old self had, she can easily hide her true feeling and argue with her own thinking.

"I thought you were looking at the kids and wish you have your own."

"You're kidding me, Em."

"Seriously, who knows you can find your man in the resort."

"Now, that was a real big joke."

"We're here!"

Their conversation was interrupted by Shane.

The van went inside the big, white gate, with a big logo of Pentagon Knights. The logo is just the shape of pentagon but there's a red eye crafted in the middle of it, it's looking straight to the eye of any person watching it, seems like trying to lure that person to get inside the resort. While each side of the pentagon has the silhouette of wine glasses and five men. It's beautiful.

So the van stopped. Everyone went out the van excitedly except her. There's something in this place. Hope she won't regret coming here, after all, she was the one who persuaded the team to pursue with the outing.

She came out of the van.

She can see that everyone is waiting outside. But her co-writers are busy admiring the place. It's Em who gave her the compliment she didn't ever want to hear.

"You look very beautiful, honey, even after the accident."

And to prove that Em is right, she saw a couple of men glancing at her. They wink at her. Smiling at her.

But she didn't glance back, nor return their smiles.

"Rob!"

It was Shane again. She sounded like an excited teenager.

She see a man walking towards their location. Sure, he's good looking, might be in his 40's. He's a foreigner, a European maybe.

Shane's husband give him a brotherly hug and Shane, too.

"I'm glad you came. I felt so sad when you said you will cancel your reservation. There's so much I want to show your team about Pentagon Knights."

"I'm sorry about that, Rob. Some inevitable circumstance sometimes happens." She knows that Shane meant about her accident. "Well, I would like you to meet my Editor, our Editor. Rob, this is Emily Higgins. And Em, this is Robert, the friend that I told you about, one of the owners of this resort."

Em gave him a kiss on the cheek. She's used to this kind of greeting.

"Hello, Em. I am happy to meet you. Indeed, your team is a group of beautiful women!"

"Thank you, Rob. Or can I call you that way?"

"Sure. And my wife said her grateful thanks for sending the books. Rowena is a faithful fan of Monica."

She heard everyone chuckled. And Victoria starting to tease her.

"Speaking of. I want you to meet my tres marias, the foundation of my team. You know Shane. And Victoria." Em started to introduce them to the man named Rob or Robert.

"Hello, Rob. I have been hearing great things about your resort. My angels would love it here. My name is Victoria."

"It's a pleasure to finally meet you in person, Victoria. I'm a fan. Your books are great."

"Ehem." Mon tried to make his presence visible.

Victoria laugh.

"This is my husband, Montemar. And he's the jealous type and that made me love this man so much."

Everyone would love Victoria, she's not only beautiful but she's also sexy.

"And I'm a great fan of Monica and Shane." A man speaks from her back. She didn't bother to turn her head.

She's starting to feel uncomfortable. Why don't they just go to the sea right away and dive?

"I'm a fan of Drei and Monica, too."

Another man joined them, speaking from her back again. Another fan of hers.

"Who among these beautiful women is Monica? I am dying to meet her?" Another voice is heard.

Define death. That's how she felt now. She feels like dying. Why does Em have to talk to these men?

Em made a very big smile.

Surely Em had no plan to introduce her to these men. But she's wrong.

"Well, gentlemen, it's time you meet the talisman of my team. The terms smart and beautiful are named after her. I have to warn you though that she's a magnet to your kind. This is Casslynn, the Monica, you admired."

She felt her face growing red.

Oh heavens, kill me now!

All four men stare at her. Speechless. Jaws drop. Including the faithful Robert.

"Wow! Oh, well, hello beautiful lady. My name is Robert. Call me Rob. I am married. And I just lost 50K today on a bet with my wife."

"Pretty, oh heavens, sexy, my name is Charlie. I am very proud to meet you, finally. I am an avid fan. I love your erotic books. Thought you are in your 40's or 50's." He gave her a sweet smile, but didn't return it back. She didn't even say a word. "I'm glad you're not."

"Unlucky, Ale-, Andrew, he didn't meet you. Beautiful lady, I'm Ben. You're indeed beautiful, wish I meet you long ago." She felt that Ben is a nice guy but just the same she didn't smile at him.

"Well, if Andrew is here, I'm sure he drag you to his car already. Pretty, my name is Franky." He tried to extend his hand but she didn't attempt to even move her hand to meet his.

"I appreciate your warm welcome for our team, but excuse my attitude, we travelled almost four hours and I feel exhausted. If you could lead us to the place where we can stay I would appreciate that." Finally, she was able to talk.

"I'm sorry. Alright, Ben would bring you to the penthouse. And Shane and Em, if you could come with me to sign some papers, please." Said Rob. He's trying not to stare at her.

"Isn't it Andrew who's supposed to guide them?" Charlie protest, sounded like jealous.

"He isn't here, unfortunately, but tell him to meet me when he arrives."

Before Ben could walk them on the way to the penthouse where they should stay, Em introduced the rest of the ladies in their team.

"I am so proud that the famous and successful team of writers in the country chose to stay in our resort." She can hear Ben's compliment. Her co-writers said thanks to him, but she didn't. She didn't even think staying in this place is a good idea at all. She's starting to feel regret. She can't have privacy in this place.

"That was a total snob of you out there, Cass." Adelaide started to talk with her when they get to their rooms.

It's indeed a penthouse. Very private. She feel like she just wants to sleep here the whole time.

"I'm not use to meeting people, Ade. The reason why I used a pen name, so people won't recognize me."

"Em is telling the truth, you're the charm of the team. Did you see how those guys admired you?" Freda agreed with Adelaide.

"Did you see how the men look at you? If I could read them very well, they are trying to get you naked, Cass." That was Jenna.

"Gross." The only thing she said. "I want to borrow your laptop, if you don't mind, Brenn."

"What? I thought this is a vacation. Why are you working again, Casslynn?" Victoria look furious. Behind her is her daughter, Sab. She heard Abby laughing with Mon outside their room.

"I am just going to review some chapters. I plan to write my next book here."

"Goodness, Casslynn. Will you please get a life? I won't let you use my laptop. We are here to unwind not to work! Excuse me, I am going to take a walk with my husband." Brenn left after yelling at her.

"Me, too, I want to see their gazebo." Adelaide walked out the door.

"I'll take a look at their pool." Carly called her husband.

"And I will take some photos. Here, hon, bring us some snacks." Drei drag her husband outside.

And next was Freda, Jenna, Victoria and Sab walking out the door.

She's alone.

Argh!

This is what she hates. When they are going out she's always left out. Single, no boyfriend, no companion. Alone.

How she wish she had died with her family long ago. What happen three years ago seemed like yesterday. She made a big mistake and she's bound to suffer the consequence of it, forever. If only she listened to her father. If only she used her brain instead of her heart.

A drop of tear fell.

Maybe she wouldn't be alone now.

Chapter 13

IT'S nine in the evening.

He just came home from a long travel. Yes, he just returned home from Dubai. He's supposed to go home three days ago but met someone and just close a business deal with him. Aside from the resort business he shared with four friends he also has buy and sell business.

'Hey baby girl
I've been watching you all day
Man that thing you got behind you is amazing
You make me want to take you out and let it rain
I know you got a man but this is what you should say

It's Leavin' again. His phone rings.
Who will call him at this hour but his friends.
It was Charlie.
"Yo."

"Man where were you? You missed to see the most beautiful creation of this world today."

"Shut up, don't start to tell him the story."

He could sense that was Ben.

"I bet Alexis would drop his jaw, too."

He thinks that was Franky.

"Stop it, Charlie. Why don't you just drag that man's ass over here?"

Now he's sure it's Rob.

"Hey, hey. What are those men murmuring in the background? Where are you, Charlie?"

"In the club, bro."

"Why Rob is still there?" He wonders. Usually Rob is already home at 7:30.

"Well, Rowena is here. Having chitchat with Monica."

Now he's confused.

"What is Rowena doing there? Are the kids there, too?"

"You bet." That was Ben.

"What's going on?" He's not sure if the resort is doing fine. First, it's a big question why Rob is still working at this hour. And second, why his wife is there? Did Rob cheat and Rowena caught him in the act? Just then he realize there's another name that Charlie mentioned.

"Who's Monica?"

There's laughter in the background.

"Hey. What are you guys laughing at?" He's tired and in no mood to play jokes at this time.

"Seriously? You don't know Monica?"

He is serious. He doesn't know anyone named Monica. Only one woman name rooted in his mind other than his mother. A thought of Casslynn appeared in his mind. He silently cursed.

"New girlfriend?" He asked ignoring the reflection of Casslynn in his mind.

"I told you, this man is not interested in writers."

He heard writers.

Something popped up in his mind.

"Are you telling me the LGP writers are there?"

"Come here, pal, and I will introduce you to Monica."

He's not interested in meeting these writers. Who are they to disturb his friends? No women ever tried to intimidate his friends. Surely not in public. But these women made Rob panic.

"I am not interested." He dryly said. "And I'm tired and sleepy."

"Are you sure you don't want to meet Monica? She's your type, bro." That was Franky.

"Nah."

"Is that a final answer? Although petite women is not my type, but this one is an exception, bro, Monica is very beautiful, she will be mine."

"Yes. And stop bugging me people."

Then he turned off his phone.

Who is this Monica?

Charlie called him again.

"Bro, I forgot to tell you, that Monica is the most after sought writer in this country other than Shane and

Victoria. Oh, that was a pen name by the way and her real name is-"

"Stop it, Charlie!" He heard Robert's voice and the call ended.

Hmmm. Most after sought.

A big word.

Interesting.

He knows one real good writer.

Casslynn.

He trusted her work so much. Too bad he didn't get the chance to read the book she wrote for him. He tried to search for Casslynn's name in the internet, but no results so far. He can't remember the title she gave him for the book, so can't look for it online either.

But this Monica.

He turned on his iPad.

Went to search her name.

He started to type book authors and add the name 'Monica' on the search box. Some suggestions appear.

..Monica bestselling author

..Monica's bestsellers'

..Monica's list of books made into film

..Monica best author from LGP

..Monica author

Wow.

So this Monica is indeed very famous.

He typed Monica and clicked on Search.

He first went to read Monica's profile.

A very short biography about her.

...Monica is an author from Love Grow Publishing. The pride of the company. Monica is writing books for more than ten years now... **Watch out for Monica's next bestselling book...**<u>click here</u> **to view current lists of Monica's book that became bestseller for all time...**

He clicked the link.

There were about more than 30 bestseller books from Monica written in less than one year.

Another wow!

This woman is impressive then.

He browse through the list of books. By the title alone he can guess that her books are erotic. One book caught his attention. The title looks familiar.

He tried to click on the preview link to get a glimpse of the story.

...Opps, preview is no longer available, <u>click here</u> **to buy a copy...**

He tried to click on the link.

..Not available, contact LGP to get a copy..

How the hell can she contact LGP then?

The book. Could it be the book Casslynn wrote for him? Did Casslynn sell the copyright of the book to LGP after she found her man? Had she really totally forgotten him?

He felt a sudden, deep sadness.

Chapter 14

SHE's having trouble sleeping again. The death of her parents and sister, it's haunting her again. How Henry fooled and hurt her, she's having the nightmare again.

She woke up sweating.

But then an image of a handsome man keep flashing her mind.

Who is he?

She heard his name in her dream.

Alexis.

That name again.

Where the hell did she hear this name?

She tried to remember but then it would only make her feel worse like her head is breaking apart.

It's 2am.

She decided to take a walk in the seashore. She hoped all people are asleep already so she can freely enjoy the sea breeze.

She put on a swimsuit just in case she decided to take some dip.

The place is beautiful indeed. You can see the lights afar. The wild Cassiopeia city can be seen from here.

She keeps walking until her feet touch the sea water. It is cold but its making her feel calm. The water made her fears and worries disappear.

How she wished her family are still alive.

Remembering how she caused their deaths made her cry again.

She then decided to soak herself in the water.

She swim here and there.

She felt tired now.

She feels like she's going to collapse.

She decided to go back to the penthouse.

Then a man standing in the seashore caught her attention.

He seemed to be shouting at her.

"Hey, lady, who told you to swim at this hour?"

When she get near to the man, she see that she's handsome.

Adonis. Perfect.

Then she felt something different inside her. Heat. But then she's soaking wet. It's about to blow her up. Her heart is beating fast, too. She cannot even blink. This man must have been in her fantasy in the past. He is the perfect definition of the word 'yummy'. She almost think of removing her swimsuit and get naked in front of this man. What's going on with her? By simply looking at this man she's starting to feel horny.

"C-Casslynn? What are you doing here?"

She was surprised. He called her by her name.

When she came nearer to him, she realized something. This man looks familiar.

"Y-you know me? Who are you?" Her head hurts. She feels like her whole body trembles. Her knees weaken.

"You have forgotten me? It's Alexis."

She just stared at him, eyes widened with unbelief.

She wants to say something but her world suddenly turns black and she feels like falling. And everything is gone.

Chapter 15

"DID an angel fall from the sky?"

She's about to open the door when she heard Shane talking.

They have two more days left to stay in Pentagon Knights, so she decided to enjoy the remaining days.

"That's crazy, Shane. Where are the others? Sleeping already?"

"Why? You are so sexy, Cass. I wish I have that lovely body. The kids are sleeping with their dad. But I will follow the others to the bar. Are you coming?"

"I would like to. Do you think my outfit is acceptable?" Ignoring her compliment.

"Oh my goodness, Casslynn, men will going to fall in line just to get your name, I bet."

"Silly, Shane. Let's go."

Just before they could reach the bar where her co-writers and Em are having some drinks a certain guy tried to approach her and Shane.

"Hey, pretty lady. Can I join you?"

She's not sure if the man is referring to her or Shane.

"Sure. I'm Shane but I'm married. My husband is sleeping with our kids."

He didn't even look disappointed.

"That's great. You don't look like a mom. I am interested with this beautiful, sexy lady, though."

"I have a date. Waiting for me inside." She lied. Wow, she could get the award of being the best liar.

Shane looked at her with brows raised.

"Let's go, Shane." She dragged her friend inside, leaving the man who now look really, really disappointed.

"Hey, Cass, what are you doing?" Shane tried to protest when she grabbed her arm leading her to the table where the ladies from LGP are sitting.

"Oh, what happened? You two look like someone is running after you." Victoria said when they reached their table.

"Well, this young lady, drag me just to avoid that young man outside." Shane answered.

"Really? Is he handsome?" Brenn asked.

"Hello, ladies. Did you enjoy the night?" The man walking towards their table is the man named Charlie. "Hi, Monica."

"Don't call me that, not here." She looked around. And surely, there are men looking at her.

"Oh, well. Don't you want people know who you are behind those books you write?"

"I intend to use my real name when I'm in public." She reasoned.

"That's a surprise." There came Franky. "I know someone who does the opposite."

She didn't smile but she look at him like she's asking what he means.

"I agree. This man just doesn't want to use his real name in public. Even we are prohibited to call him his real name. I guess no one really know his real name but us." Ben just joined them followed by Robert and his wife Rowena.

"I hope my friends are enjoying this night. Just order anything you want here. This is the resort's complementary to celebrities." Said Robert.

"And hey, Monica, see this." Rowena showed her a photo of her compilation of her books. She felt proud. But then a little bit disappointed. Rowena just called her by her pen name.

"No one was looking out the counter. Why all of you are here? Do you intend to have me watch the bar the entire night? I have not recovered from fatigue and jetlag from my travel yet."

She heard a very irritated voice behind her. She turn back and was surprised to see the man talking.

"Alexis?"

"Casslynn?"

Yes, she remembered him now. Alexis, she remembered everything now. Everything. Including what happened two days ago. The presence of Alexis just made her blushed.

What she didn't realize is the unbelievable look from the faces of four men in front of her including Rowena.

"How did you know Andrew's real name?" All five of them asked in chorus.

This time, she saw how Alexis blushed.

"You know this guy?" Altogether the ladies from LGP asked her.

"How did you meet Casslynn?" Again the four men asked Alexis in chorus.

"Wait." She and Alexis said at the same time. "Ops." They said again at the same time.

"Alright, you go first." Alexis said smiling.

She didn't smile back. Not when she's surrounded with people with questions in their faces.

"Well, yeah. I met him two days ago. In the beach." That's partly true. Of course she can't tell them that Alexis had been a friend for a long time and most especially her co-writers don't have to know that Alexis is the man in her book. Most of all, no one should know what happen to them two days ago

But not Em. Em's look is full of uncertainty. Casslynn knows she has a lot of explaining to make later.

"Yeah. Same here." Said Alexis who is now seriously staring at her.

She feel a little awkward.

"Okay." Almost everyone chorused. But she knows they are just pretending to believe them. Of course her answer is not believable either.

Chapter 16

"I thought you will deny me."

"Agh! Shoot." She just got her butt hit the coconut tree behind her. Hearing the voice of the man talking at her back almost made her leaped.

"Did I make you surprised?" He said while sipping through the soda can he's holding.

"A bit." She felt her face getting red again. Why does this man always make her uncomfortable.

"You didn't answer me." He's staring at her like looking through her soul.

She didn't answer him. "How did you know I'm here?"

"I'm one of the owners of this resort, Casslynn." He simply said without getting his eyes off her.

"Can you stop staring at me?" She frowned.

"Why? I never thought I would see you one day. Much more sleeping with you." Alexis said.

She stared at him full of aggravation.

But he just smiled at her.

A smile that made her remember what happen two days ago.

She woke up a little dizzy. She's trying to figure out what happen.

"I am glad you're awake, ganda."

A handsome man burst out from the door.

No! This can't be.

"A-alexis?"

"Oh I am glad you remember me now. Back there in the shore, I was hurt thinking why you have forgotten me that easily."

"What happen?" The only thing she can say.

"I was doing a round check of the entire resort when I saw a woman coming up from the sea. Thought I saw a beautiful mermaid. I was surprised to see you. Finally, meeting you." He said with amazement.

"I was just trying to get some fresh air but the water is tempting. Where am I?" She rose from lying in the bed. She just noticed that the bed is large. It can occupy two persons.

"You're still inside the Pentagon Knights but in my cabin." He smiled at her while caressing her hair. It made her jolt that she almost fell from the bed. "I'm sorry. Did I startle you, ganda? I always wanted to do this."

"Not really." Just then she realized she's no longer wearing the same one-piece suit she had. "Where's my wet suit? W-who undressed me?"

He looked at her full of amusement.

"I undressed you, ganda."

Her eyes widened with disbelief after hearing him.

"W-what?" She even stammered. "Why did you do it? Then you see m-me n-naked." She felt so ashamed of what this guy did.

"I have seen all of you, ganda. You're perfect. I was tempted to touch and kiss you but I waited until you're fully awake." He gave a wicked smile. "Oh, I love to see your hand touching me there."

Just then she realized her right hand is placed right on top of his male member. What made her quiver is the realization that this man is hard. Having a real bad hard on that his boxer looks like making a very tall tent.

She felt herself blushed to the extent level.

"I love it when you blushed. It made me wanted to kiss you." His voice now sounded really very sexy. He didn't wait for her to say a word. He kissed her.

His lips is moist and warm.

To him, her lips tastes like his favorite cherry cake.

He stop kissing her for few seconds then look at her face again.

"I can't believe you're real. You have a very beautiful face, ganda." Then he kissed her again.

This time the kiss went deeper. He tastes her tongue. Bite her lips a little and suck it.

The kiss lasted few minutes. They both have hard time catching their breath.

"You're very handsome."

"Thank you, ganda. Can I see more of you?"

She just smiled.

Shit!

She heard him curse.

"Why?" She asked, confused.

"Your smile made me even grow hard. Look." The next thing he does made her eyes grow even wider and made her feel wet inside.

Alexis pulled out his penis inside his boxer. She had seen it before, it was enormous and beautiful. But today seeing it bare and naked, made her realize it's beyond enormous and beautiful. It's very beautiful and by the looks of it she knows she will die.

"Would you like to touch 'him', ganda?" He asked still looking in her eyes.

"Will 'he' bite me?" She tried to make a joke to disregard the horny feeling she has inside.

She's surprise that he laugh at her joke.

"No, ganda. But I will."

Without hesitation she touch his male member. It's indeed very hard. But what's shameful is her small hand, she can't hold it in full. Indeed he is huge. She was tempted to kiss the shiny, pink head.

"Don't suck it, ganda, 'he' will choke you."

"It's yummy, Alexis."

"Do you like 'him' big and hard?"

"Are you kidding me? I love it super big and hard." She sounded pissed.

Alexis just laugh at her.

"You said it so sexy, ganda." It made her eyebrows raised. It only made Alexis laugh again.

"Mmmmm, your balls..." She can't believe he had very big balls.

"Told you, they're big."

She kissed his balls, too, just like what he wanted her to do before. And she kissed his big gun again, tastes it with her tongue. Tried to put it inside her mouth, but half of it won't even fit there. She felt like choking.

Alexis moaned.

"Oh, Casslynn, ganda, love what you're doing to 'him'."

She continued sucking 'him'. She felt a little sticky liquid coming from its head, it tastes a little salty but she like it.

"Oh ganda, stop it. You will get choked. Come here." *Then he started undressing her. She must be wearing his T-shirt because it looks like she's wearing a gown. Alexis is a big man. He must be over six feet.*

She didn't know she only has T-shirt without anything underneath.

"You're beautiful, Casslynn."

Then he started kissing her on the mouth again. It was another long, deep kiss before he move his mouth slowly down to her neck. Now she knows how a vampire bite feels, she can feel his lip marks on her neck.

His mouth seemed to have its own mind because now his moving down to her breasts. Slowly kissing each tip.

She felt a little shy. Tried to pull his head so he won't kiss her there.

"Why?" *He asked, sounded irritated.*

"I have small breasts."

"No, they are not. They are perfect for my mouth and hands. See this?" *He cup one breast in one hand and the other with his remaining hand. Squeeze each one with care, like he is trying to pick a fruit from its tree.*

He sucked each nipple like a hungry baby. He bit each tip like he is eating an ice cream.

While his mouth is busy exploring her breasts, his hand now started to move down, to her thighs, then it stopped right there in the middle.

"Shit! Casslynn, you have a very beautiful vagina! Are you sure you slept with your ex?" He asked with astonishment.

"Yes, I slept with Henry couple of times. Why?" It's a surprised that the mention of Henry's name no longer hurts.

"Well, your vagina doesn't look like a male member had explored her couple of times. 'She' looked fresh and virgin." He said without lifting his eyes from looking at her feminine flower.

That only made her feel even wet.

He kissed her there. He licked her wet hole now.

"Mmmmm you tastes good." Then he bit her clit a little while thrusting one finger inside.

Shit! She felt a little pain. Alexis has a big finger and she had no sex for three years now.

"Alexis stop."

But he didn't hear her. He continued to thrust one finger while licking and sucking her. Just like what he told her before, he touch her feminine flower while sucking his cherry pop pop.

"Please..." She begged. Not to stop him. But to signal him to do more.

He slowly positioned her.

She opened her legs wide.

"Are you ready to welcome 'him'?"

"Yes. I hope I won't die."

He chuckled.

Slowly he thrusts his big gun.

Sure, it hurts.

He tried to stop.

"Stop and you will die." She glared at him.

He laugh a little.

Finally, he completely thrusts inside.

A single tear fall from her eyes. Then she scream his name when he started to move.

"Alexisss.."

He suddenly stop.

"Why?" She wonder why.

"Did you just say my name?" He looked surprise.

"Should not I?" She's puzzled.

"No. I love it."

But what Alexis realized is that no woman in his past had said his name when he fucked her, only Casslynn. She said it with full conviction like she's telling him that he is hers.

"Please go on, Alexis. And faster, please."

He obediently did what she asked him.

She's very tight. But Alexis like it. He truly believes that this woman had not slept to any man after her stupid ex left her.

"Oh, Alexis, oh."

He couldn't count how many times she had said his name.

"Oh, Casslynn."

What he didn't realize is that he just exploded inside her. Inside her. No condom, no protection. But his sperm freely swim inside her.

"I hate it that you left me on that day after our love making."

She was back to reality. She heard him but she won't make it a big deal.

"Why are you here? You should be helping your friends running the resort." She said, not paying attention to what he is saying.

He tried to pull her, tried to look at her face.

"Are you avoiding me?"

She tried to fight him. She looked at him, too, but she's sure Alexis can't read her true feelings.

"I am not. But I came here for legitimate business."

"Is that why you didn't tell your friends we know each other way back. How long have it been? Three, four months?"

"We were just chat friends, Alexis. Don't make it a big deal."

She thought its pain she saw in his eyes?

But she's wrong.

"LOL. You're so serious, *ganda*. I am just trying to make you." He laugh like nothing happened.

"Hmp! I am short in patience, Alexis. Don't make me." She said while walking away from him.

"Hey, wait. Can we just talk?"

"About what?" She asked while continued walking.

"Why are you with the writers from LGP?"

She stop walking and look at him like he is some kind of idiot.

"Seriously, you don't know?"

"I wouldn't ask you if I know, *ganda*."

"Goodness. Okay. Let me tell you. These writers are here to unwind. Should not be if Monica didn't insists for the team to come here."

"Wow. So this Monica really is very famous and influential. Who among them is Monica?"

She looked at him again, now really feeling annoyed.

"Alexis. I am Monica."

She saw him dropping his jaw. Speechless. Like his asleep but awake. Define enchanted. That's Alexis, he looks like someone had cast a spell on him and gets him enchanted.

"I-i can't believe you're Monica!" What he said after returning to his physical world.

"How does it look like there?" She joked.

"What?" He asked looking like stupid.

"I'm just kidding you, you looked like you just returned from the enchanted kingdom."

"Ah, silly. I just can't believe I am talking to a famous writer at this point."

"Shhh." She stopped him.

"Why?"

"I don't want anyone here to know my author name. I am happy that people know me as Casslynn."

"Hmmm. So humble."

She just smiled at him.

Shit!

She heard him cursed.

She wonder why.

"You made me hard again."

Shit! This time, she can stop from cursing, too.

"Maybe you can do something." He chuckled. He's telling her they will have sex again.

"Not now, not here, Alexis." She firmly said.

"Oh." He looked disappointed.

"I don't want my friends and Em get suspicious on me."

"I don't know what you mean by that. But I am just wondering. Did you find your man yet, *ganda*?"

"Not yet, Alexis."

Chapter 17

H E whistled. Sounded so happy. He woke up this morning feeling like he is floating. He is on rest day today. But here he comes at work even earlier than the security guard on duty.

"I can't believe you're here. I thought the guard was lying when he said that Mr. Andrews is already in. What's wrong with you, bro?"

That was Charlie. And following him is Franky.

Sure the owners of this resort are womanizers except for Robert, but they take their business seriously. Charlie and Franky normally come in the office early.

"You're supposed to be off-duty, bro. We don't need your ass here today." Said Franky.

"Silly, men. You should get worry if I don't come in to work." He answered without looking at them. He was busy checking the list for reservations today. He found out they have lots of voicemails and emails to return. "What do we have for today's meal?"

The two men stared at him like he is possessed. Then Charlie said something.

"I didn't know you love classic love songs, bro. What's that, Chicago? You're The Inspiration? Sucks!"

"What's the problem with Chicago? I love that band and their songs are great."

"Oh? You look inspired, bro. Is it Casslynn? Or do you call her Monica?" Franky teased him.

"You, silly men, stop it and just do your job." If he is in bad mood today he could have shouted at them. But he's not. And yes, he is inspired. It's because of Casslynn.

"You must be in love with her already." Charlie still won't leave the topic off.

He's startled.

"Of course not. You know me. I don't believe in that stupid word." *Casslynn is great in bed*. He wanted to tell them. Casslynn is not the girlfriend type. Falling in love with her will never happen.

"Don't you think it's time you settle down, bro?" Franky seriously asked him.

"Whoa, whoa. Look who's talking. You guys are getting far. You know that I am not the marrying type." He raised his hands like telling them to close the topic.

They shake their heads, showing sign of surrender.

"Okay. If that's what you believe. I hope you won't regret it in the end." Franky said.

"What do you mean?"

"C'mon, you know what Franky means. Casslynn is a very pretty woman, a smart one. You can't find anyone like her. But someone like you bro, too many to count." Then both Charlie and Franky went on their way to the counter.

He was left thinking.

Charlie's words echoed in his mind.

You can't find anyone like her. But someone like you, too many to count.

The words just keep repeating in his mind.

Shit!

He is not going to lose Casslynn, is he?

Chapter 18

"THERE'S a package for Casslynn."

Everyone heard the security guard talking over the intercom.

Not only her teammates are teasing her but she also heard laughs of writers from other teams who are present in their office today.

"Wow, Cass, is that package from-"

"Shut up, Shane." She cut her off.

Ever since they returned from Pentagon Knights, ever since Alexis told them they are friends, her co-writers had been teasing her. They greeted him about having a boyfriend finally.

"Oh I was about to say that the package came from your boyfriend, Cass." Shane continued teasing her.

"How am I supposed to make you believe ladies that Alexis is not my boyfriend. He is not even the dating type." That is true. Sure, they had sex, a pretty good one. But they are just sex partners, nothing else.

"But why? You and Alexis look good together. And you have no idea how Alexis stare at you. He likes you a lot, Cass." Victoria added.

"Victoria is right. I am even tempted to write a story about you, Cass. Maybe it's time that Monica should fall in love and a perfect book must be written." Adelaide agreed.

"Argh! You married ladies are writers indeed. What I wrote will not happen in real life. That's why they are called stories." If only they know what's the real score between him and Alexis. Ah she knows Em will kill her.

"Hmmm. Why do I have this feeling that your book released during the anniversary special is written after Alexis? You know, it's a coincidence that Alexis met Lynn in a beach resort. And it's another coincidence that you name your characters Alexis and Lynn." Brenn just came in with a box of pizza.

"Your imaginations are working very well, ladies of Em. I bet each of you could finish one story today." She just smiled, which made the rest of the women go 'ohhhh'. "I will go downstairs and pick up this package."

On her way to the reception desk where packages and other items are received, she met other writers.

"Hey, Casslynn, I heard you have a boyfriend. I bet he didn't propose yet." It's Destiny, known for her rhyme words and some say it's a prophecy about you and a prophecy always come true.

"Not now, Destiny. Please." She sounded like begging. The last thing she wanted to hear from Destiny is her prophecy of rhyme words.

"Don't worry darling. The sun will go down and meet the moon, stars will be shown. One day, the sun will go away. What will matter is your laughter. Tear will always be there, but never fear as for you will be a happy ever after." Then off she goes.

Creepy. Sometimes she wonder why LGP got a writer like Destiny. She's a bit off, closer to becoming crazy.

"Did she speak to you with those rhyme words, too?" That was Jenna.

"Yes. It sounded so creepy." She honestly said, after signing the receipt upon claiming her package.

"Do you know that they come true?" Jenna continued.

"Excuse me?" She's not sure if she heard her right.

"She gave me rhyme words, too, when I came here. Right inside the elevator. I didn't know her then, but her words sound so creepy that it got stuck in my mind. I even have nightmares about it. But after few years her words came true and now I have Jonas." Jenna smiled.

"Your case is different, Jenn. I can't even remember exactly what she said." It's a lie. She can still say those words how Destiny had said them.

But whatever it means, will never happen.

Chapter 19

"Missed you, *ganda*. I plan to pick you up after work but I thought you won't like it. Give me a call if you want me to meet you there. Otherwise, I will see you in your place."**

It was the message on the package. When she opened it, it was a box of chocolate and a little card with a name. It's that little card from a flower shop.

Is Alexis trying to court her?

Don't be a fool, Casslynn!

She told herself as the realization awakens that Alexis will never take a woman seriously.

She drop by the said flower shop on the way to her apartment. When she reached the place she was surprised that a female attendee recognized her.

"We are waiting for you, Ms. Casslynn. Alexis said you will be here in matter of time. This flower is for you."

It's a bouquet of tulips. Variety of tulips.

She almost leaped with joy.

How did Alexis know about her favorite flower?

She was still day dreaming when she reached her apartment.

But what she saw when she's about to open the gate is the person she never expected.

"Alexis!" She was surprised to see him waiting in the gate.

"Hello, *ganda*. Did you like the flower?" He said smiling at her.

"I'm surprised you're here. And yes, I like the flower. How did you know I love tulips?" She told him, not looking at him. "Come inside." She invited him inside her apartment, didn't even think what would happen when she is alone with him.

"Well, I browse through books that you wrote and I noticed that in every book your author name always have this tulips flower design, I figure you love tulips."

He followed her inside.

How smart! She wonders how many people notice the same thing that Alexis did.

"You're a keen observant."

"Not as smart as you, though." As soon as he is inside her apartment, he sit on the couch as if he owns the apartment. "This is a nice place. I like the scent of your home, so feminine, so you."

"Should I thank you for that compliment?" She smiled at him without thinking of its effect to Alexis. Next thing she heard is him cursing.

Too late for her to realize that Alexis grabs her and sit her on his lap.

"You know that I don't like you smiling at me that way." He started to nibble her ear.

"I forgot. A-alexis, please." She started to feel the fire raging inside her that only Alexis can extinguish.

"Please, what, *ganda*?" It is not a question but a warning that he will do more than just nibbling her ear.

She felt his hardness. She felt his big gun moving inside his pants.

He started kissing her. From forehead to the tip of her nose, to her cheeks down to her lips. And he stayed there. As if trying to savor the taste of her mouth.

And the obedient Casslynn as she is, she opened her mouth trying to welcome the little visitor. Meeting his tongue with hers.

They are both catching their breath.

"I can't get enough of you. Do you know that?"

"Hmmmm. How many women did you sleep with lately?"

"Hmmmm. Honestly, I didn't sleep with another woman since meeting you. Well, why should I, you alone can already drain my entire energy, I have nothing left for another woman."

"Is that true?" She asked like a jealous girlfriend.

"Are you jealous?" He teased him while trying to give her small kisses on the cheek.

"Are you courting me?" She's not supposed to ask him. But she doesn't understand why he give her the chocolate and flower.

"If this is about the flower, no *ganda*, I still want you to be my bestfriend. Girlfriends dump you when they are over with their men, and I hate to think of you dumping me. We better stay as friends. Don't you think?"

If this is Henry she could have hit him already, shouted at him. But this is Alexis. And he is right, they better stay as friends... with benefits, she guessed.

"Well, you have the point. But I am really hungry. Do you mind helping me in the kitchen?"

"With a little pay, yes." He gave her wicked smile.

"What payment?" She felt nervous.

He kissed her on the lips again. It was a quick French kiss that made her catch her breath again.

"Naughty."

"Just a kiss for now, *ganda*. But after eating, I want to see your room with a naked goddess sitting in the middle of the bed."

"You have no plan to sleep here, do you?"

"Actually, I was just about to ask you if I can."

"If you can wash the dishes."

"If you will give me support by hugging me and pressing your breasts from my back."

"Naughty." She poke his nose before heading hurriedly to the kitchen. She heard him giving a loud laugh.

Chapter 20

"How was your day?"

She's resting on Alexis' arm. They just finished the second round of their love making. And they are having some chitchats. Talking about what happen to their day.

"It was pretty good. I don't usually go to the office except if it's last week of the month and if I'm bored. Yours?"

"Kinda busy. I need to return couple of voicemails and emails. But the entire day I have been thinking of you."

She just smiled at him, which is another wrong move because now Alexis cursed again. And the next thing he did, he moved to lie with his back putting her on top of him.

"Now, what did I tell you about smiling, *ganda*?"

"I forgot."

"Wrong answer. Kiss me again."

Without waiting a second, she kissed him on the lips. This time she gave him little bites.

"That's so sweet."

She forced his mouth to open. After successfully opening the portal before the gates of heaven, she touched his tongue with his. While her hand secretely touches his enormous male member. She heard him moan.

While sitting on top of him she saw how he stared at her breasts. Without waiting her command his mouth grab one nipple and suck it. This time, she heard herself moan.

"Casslynn, you're making me crazy." His mouth continued sucking one nipple to another.

She continued to slide his manhood with her hand. He continued to moan.

She can't help but pulled his hair.

Shit!

He switched their positions. She is now lying under him.

He stared at her for few seconds.

"What?"

"You are very beautiful. No man can ever resists your beauty."

"Stop talking and fuck me, Alexis." All she could say. But she wish he would just love her. Marry her and... She can't say it.

He positioned on top of her.

Then slowly, he slide his big gun inside his delicate feminine hole.

Somehow, there's still a little hurt she felt when he completely pushed inside. The little pain will always be there as long as Alexis remains big and hard.

He pushed just slowly. While squeezing her breasts. Giving her small kisses.

The Alexis move, as she called it.

Alexis is heavy but she doesn't care. She loves to feel his weight on her.

"*Ganda*, do you want me to move faster now?"

Alexis always respect her. Whatever he does, he always ask her opinion or decide for it.

"Please, handsome. Drive me crazy."

He did as she commanded.

He push and pull faster now. She could feel her breath running short. He is grasping some air.

But they continued. Heat against heat. Fire is racking inside their bodies. She never felt this kind of blast only Alexis can ignite. The bomb has been detonated. But there's a timer. Casslynn knows it would take couple of minutes for Alexis to explode.

"I'm almost there." He warned her.

"Oh, Alexis, baby, please." She almost plead.

"I'm cumming. Oh."

"Alexisss."

And they reach the doors of heaven together.

They could make a good porn video.

"I love you." Her mouth just said it without her control.

Alexis looked at her for a moment. But didn't say anything.

Did he hear her say the words? May he didn't. Did he just ignored her? Maybe, maybe, he's just really interested with sex. Just sex, no emotions.

"Let's sleep now. Come, place your head in my arm. I will hug you, *ganda*."

What else could she do?

She did as he instructed her.

Then she closed her eyes.

Alexis is left staring at the ceiling.

He heard her. She said the forbidden words he never wanted to hear again.

I'm sorry, Casslynn. But I can't love you back.

I would still wish you find the right man.

He kissed her goodnight. And plan how he can stop Casslynn from seeing him again.

Chapter 21

IT'S been a week. No calls, no messages, nothing. She wonder what happen to Alexis.

"Are you coming with us, Cass?" It's payday. Her team normally go out for dinner. But she doesn't feel like going out.

"I just want to sleep at home, Brenn. Just tell, Em."

"Oh okay. But are you alright? You look pale."

"I'm sick. I think just a little sunshine and I'll be fine."

"Fine. Enjoy your day, Cass." And Brenn left her alone.

Hopefully she would enjoy this day. She has no idea how to. She's about to turn off her computer when she got a call from the receptionist.

"Cass, could you please take the call at line 2? There's a caller looking for you."

She pick up the phone.

"Hey, *ganda*. Why are you not answering your phone?"

She's surprised to hear his voice.

"Alexis?"

"Yes. Sorry if I called you from this line. I don't know how to contact you, you're not answering your phone, not even returning my messages."

"Oh, shit. I'm sorry." She realize that she brought her office phone and left her personal phone at home. "All this time I thought I'm carrying my personal phone. I even wonder why you didn't call me. Thought you already dump me."

"Silly. Why would I do that?"

She didn't answer.

"I can't come to fetch you at work. Can you get a cab to Pentagon Knights? Other guys are not in and I may need to watch the counter 'till 9."

And it's almost 7.

"I don't see why I need to do that."

There's a silence from Alexis' end. She heard him trying to say the right words.

"Well, we have not seen each other for a week. I guess, we could spend some time together. I want you to spend a day in my condo."

'I never invited any woman in my condo, *ganda*.'

Alexis said this to her before. But why is he inviting me now?

"*Ganda*?"

"Okay, I will get a cab."

"Alright. I will wait for you."

As soon as she hung up, she get her bag and hurried outside to get to the elevator.

Good thing there's a cab parked outside their building. "Where, Maam?"

"Andromeda, please. Pentagon Knights."

Andromeda is a four-hour travel from Cassiopeia city if you take a bus. And if you are not an employee of LGP no one would take you there by cab, it's very expensive.

But the cab driver didn't even complain. He drive without any word.

She looked at herself in the mirror.

Yeah, Brenn is right, she's a little pale. But she didn't put on a makeup. She just put on a little lip gloss, cherry flavor, Alexis' favorite. Spray some perfume, also cherry scent. How did she know that Alexis loves cherry? Once Alexis asked her to buy a cherry cake, cherry apple drink and a cherry flavored yoghurt. A smart person can guess that he loves cherry.

She listened to some of Alexis' favorite music. Chicago. Silly, she doesn't like classic band. But Alexis made her listen to Chicago.

She checked her emails and answered few from her avid fans. She laugh at one email. The sender asked how many kids she has and how long had she been married. If only her readers would know that she's not even in a relationship. Kids? Silly, she doesn't want one. Maybe one day when she's already married. But getting married? She doubt it. After Alexis she doesn't know if she can still trust another man.

Another email from a male fan expresses regret. Said how he wish to meet her in person, court her and marry her, if she's not old. That made her really laugh out loud. The driver glanced at her.

She was busy checking her emails when the driver asked her.

"Maam, do you want to get inside the resort?"

"What?" She then realize they already reached Pentagon Knights. And there outside she saw Alexis standing.

"Don't have to." She paid the driver. And get off the cab. She walked towards Alexis. He is busy looking for someone he didn't notice her.

"Waiting for someone, Sir?" She changed her voice to someone really flirty.

"I'm not interested woman." His response without looking at her.

"I'm free tonight. I believe they have plenty of rooms inside the resort." Still trying to flirt with him.

"No, thanks." Still he is busy looking or maybe waiting for someone. "Oh Casslynn, what's taking you so long. You should be here by now." He sound like mumbling. But she heard him.

"You are waiting for, Casslynn?"

He is no longer paying attention to what she says.

He get his phone and tried to call someone. Just then her phone rings. He automatically looked at her direction.

"*G-ganda?*" He was surprised to see her.

She made a loud laugh making him rankle. Then he walked away.

"C'mon, Alexis, I was just kidding you." She said after following him to the parking lot.

"Don't do that again. I thought you were some kind of flirt or whore trying to get my attention."

She laugh again.

"I thought you saw me. And seeing you standing there, I thought you were waiting for someone."

"Silly. Come here." He grab her. And right then and there he kissed her torridly. Didn't mind if people are passing by. "And by laughing at me you will get a punishment later. Get in." He said after letting go of her lips. He opened the door of the passenger side of his car for her.

"Wow! Is this is a Lamborghini?" She asked with amazement, also trying to distract herself from the familiar heat she felt inside.

"Yes. Her name is Medusa. Fasten your seatbelt, *Ganda.*" He start the engine and drove off.

Chapter 22

IT took them 30 minutes to reach Alexis' condo. It was a nice place. It doesn't look like a condo because you can see that there is a garden place to plant something. There's a small fountain. And she see a vision of kids playing around the fountain.

Shit!

She cursed. The last thing she wanted is a kid.

"We're here. I hope you like my place, *ganda.*" Alexis opened the door for her. She likes the place. She never imagined him being a gentleman.

"Your place is great. But I don't understand why you call it a condo. It's a house. A beautiful one."

"Ha ha. Right. Rob said the same thing. But I just want to call this a condo. Come, let's get inside. I'm hungry I could eat you here."

She looked at him with fierce.

"Now, now, I'm just kidding you, *ganda*. If you don't mind I want you to cook for me. I bought some groceries earlier and stuck them in my fridge. But I'm a disaster in the kitchen, so I figure maybe you can help."

She marched to the door.

She almost leaped with surprised when he hugged her from behind kissing her nape.

"Pervert." She said while laughing.

"I know. And I bet you like me being pervert." He just continued nibbling her nape.

"I would like it. But Mr. Yummy if you don't let go of me, we will not be able to get inside the house and I won't be able to cook. I'm also hungry but I don't want to eat a giant."

"A handsome, yummy giant, *ganda*."

She hurriedly went inside his house. She heard him laughing. She can't help but smile, too.

She found his kitchen clean.

Hmmm. Impressive.

She had this thinking that no man can keep his kitchen neat and clean. But Alexis is different.

After seeing his kitchen, she went to check his restroom, it was clean, too.

She was tempted to go upstairs and checked his bedroom. And she did.

Well, his bedroom is very organized. It smells good, too. And his dresser is not messy.

"Satisfied?"

"Oh." He was there standing at the door, smiling at her. "A little." All she could say.

"Hmmm. So wifey." From her peripheral vision, she can see him walking towards her. And the next thing he did, he hold her from the waist. Lift her and sit her on his lap.

"I thought you're hungry." She tried to push him but he is slowly undressing her now. As quick as he can, he grab her breast and place one nipple to his mouth.

"I am. But I prefer to eat you first." He kissed her, as usual, a torrid kiss. "I wonder what kind of toothpaste you use or what you have eaten today."

"Why?" She felt embarrassed. Surely this man is not saying she has a bad breath.

"I can't get enough of you. Your mouth always taste like cherry. It's addictive."

That made her released a sexy laugh.

"And yours is just the same, handsome. Now kiss me again before I change my mind." Which he did.

After he had enough of her mouth, he then move to her breasts and engulf his face there for few minutes.

While still sitting on the bedside, Alexis removed her panty. He raised her left leg and placed it on his shoulder while he buried his face there in the middle of her thigh.

"Alexis, please." To Alexis, it's a sign of her telling him to go on.

"I love your sensitive area here, *ganda*. Making me crazy. I love your scent, your taste, so virginal."

"Ahh." She moan when he thrusts one finger while he run his tongue to her clit. "Alexis, ohh." She never expected this intense sensual feeling. Henry never made her feel this way. He continued thrusting. Kissing. Sucking her. She's lost. Lost in the wild planet of Alexis. Her world seems to be flooded with hearts. She's floating. It's heaven.

"You're so wet. I love it, *ganda*."

Right there, while Alexis is still sitting on the bedside. He pushed 'him' inside.

She still feel the same small pain. But then Alexis has his way of giving her the pleasure she needs.

She turns into a wilder woman. She scream his name so loud.

And Alexis just love it when she's screaming his name.

Just like their usual lovemaking, they both reached the heaven together.

"You're great, *ganda*."

"And you are perfect, Alexis. I think I have a new name for you."

"Really? What is it?"

"Yummy."

"Ohh."

"Can I call you that from now on?"

"I would love it, *ganda*."

"Perfect. Now, really I am hungry. You should help me in the kitchen since you already drain all my energy."

He laugh again.

His laughter is like a music to her ears.

Chapter 23

SHE'S back in Alexis' house again.

Since the last time they made love in his house, Alexis made it a routine that she should be staying in his house during weekend and during weekdays Alexis will stay in her house in Python. The arrangement cost so much money, but Alexis doesn't mind as long as he can see the beautiful writer.

It's been two weeks now that they had such routine. They almost visited all the wonderful places in the province. Every time they get to spend overnight in one place Alexis never missed a moment to make love to her. Lovemaking has been part of their daily activity. And Alexis is the type who never gets tired, so does she.

But tonight is different. After all the outdoor activities they did today, they only had one round and both slumped to bed afterwards.

She was awakened by a cellphone ring. It played the song of Jesse McCartney. She's not sure why her phone ringtone was changed, but she answered it.

"H-ello." Her eyes are still closed.

"Who are you?" Said the voice from the other line. She's not sure if it's a male or female, she's too sleepy to recognize the voice.

"Silly. You called at this hour just to ask me that. This is Casslynn, of course. Look, if-"

"Casslynn? The writer Monica?" Now she might be hearing it wrong, but the voice sounded surprised

"Uh huh. I'm really sleepy. What do you need? Can you send me an email instead? I will check it tomorrow." Still trying to stop her eyes from closing again or the phone will drop on her face.

"I am actually looking for Alexis. Just want to ask him if he can come in early tomorrow. But I guess he can't." She seemed to be hearing the voice chuckled.

"Okay. I will tell Alexis. But next time, call his phone and not mine."

"Lady, this is Alexis' number I'm calling. You-" But the next thing the man heard was a snore, a woman snoring to sleep. And the man expresses an amusing smile. No other than, Robert.

*****

Early in the morning, Alexis was awakened by Jesse McCartney's song "Leavin'".

When he checked who's calling early in the morning, it was Robert.

"Yo. It's early in the morning, Rob."

"Man, its 10AM. Do you call it early?"

He checked the wall clock and realize its 10:15 in the morning.

"Holy shit, Rob. I didn't know it's late in the morning."

"I know. A man will not really know the time if a beautiful woman is sleeping beside him." He heard him teasing.

"What?"

"If Casslynn didn't answer my call late evening last night, I wouldn't know that she's the reason why you were busy in the past two weeks or so."

His eyes widened.

"What? Casslynn? How-"

"She answered my call, bro, thinking she answered her own phone. But that's fine. I just wonder, for the first time you invited a woman inside your house." Now, he really heard him cackle.

"Rob-"

"It's okay, bro. I'm happy that finally you found a woman, and not just a woman, that's Casslynn."

"Give me few minutes to take shower and I will be there in 45 minutes." He changed the topic.

"Don't bother. Ben will cover for you today. I told the guys."

"Holy shit, Robert. You didn't."

"I did. And Charlie said he saw you two times with Casslynn. You are not simply with Casslynn, but you had her ride Medusa. You've changed bro, I thought no woman can ride your lovely Lamborghini, not even us are allowed to ride her."

Oh, he's doomed.

Knowing his friends, they will tease him for sure.

Oh, Casslynn, it seems that you are starting to mess up with my life. But he just saw her snoring.

She's sleeping peacefully. She's really beautiful. If this is a different time of his life, maybe he just wants to stay there and stare at her until she wakes up. Remembering how Robert tease him, he started to dislike the idea of having Casslynn in his condo, or house as they said it is.

"Hmmm. Alexis?" She's awake now. "How long have I been sleeping?"

"Almost whole day. Now, wake up, Casslynn, we have to go."

She stiffened.

"Are you mad?"

"No, but it's late. I need to go to work and you need to go back to the city."

"I don't need to. I can write here. I can use your laptop."

"No, don't use my things."

"Wait a minute, Alexis. Do we have a problem? Why do I have this feeling that you have a bad morning."

"You answered Robert's call last night. You should not touch my phone."

"I didn't. It was my phone I answered."

"Can you not remember anything?"

Just then her eyes widened.

"Holy crap. So that's why the ringtone was different. If it was Robert-"

Her eyes widened again as the realization came to her.

"Oh my goodness. So Robert knows I have been sleeping here and-"

"Precisely."

"I need to go back to the city then." But before she can even get up to fix herself, her world starting to rock. Her vision becomes blurry. She felt like she's about to throw up.

"Are you okay?" From slightly furious to worried, Alexis asked her.

"I'm going to throw up." She rushed to the rest room right away. There in the sink she vomit.

Alexis followed her.

It took her few minutes to release everything.

"You look pale." Alexis now felt worried but a new feeling came in, nervous, fear.

"I'm fine. I think I still need to get some rest." She felt her knees weakened. When she tried to walk she almost fell. So Alexis need to carry her to the bed.

They were both staring at nothing when Alexis asked.

"How many days have you been delayed?"

She was shocked.

"God! I'm not-"

Shit! Shit!

She heard him curse.

"You're pregnant."

Chapter 24

SHE has not answered to any of Em's calls or from anyone. She is also not in the mood to write anything. A week ago Alexis and she confirmed her pregnancy.

The last thing she wanted to happen is to get pregnant. God! Why?

How can she handle pregnancy alone? She doesn't want to be a single mother. Long ago she wished to have a kid. After knowing how complicated her dream was, she stopped dreaming about having a kid, husband or even a family.

How the hell am I going to get out from this situation?

She cried again. She can't count how much tears she had shed since knowing about her pregnancy. She didn't talk to the father of her child as well.

Her child.

She felt a little creeps.

She needs to get rid of this pregnancy.

Abortion is an option. But can she afford to kill another life? Her family's death was her fault. It's as if she's the one who killed them.

*****

Alexis on the other hand had not been sleeping better since a week that he had last seen Casslynn. After learning her pregnancy he was bothered. Not because he had made a mistake. Yes, that little thing that Casslynn had in her uterus is a mistake. Not because he is worried about marrying her. Hell, he will not marry Casslynn just because she's pregnant.

He is worried because he had caused Casslynn a really big trouble. How on earth can Casslynn find her dream man now that he got her pregnant?

Most of all, how in the world can he get rid of what she's about to bring into the world in about 9 months or so?

'Shit! Shit!' He pound the table while cursing.

"You look like carrying the whole world, bro. What's the problem? Women? Is it Casslynn? Did she try to stop your womanizing habit now? I told you she's-"

"Will you please shut up, Robert?!?" He yelled at him.

"Opps. Looks like you are really having a bad day. I don't mean to be nosy, but I know Casslynn is the faithful type. I can see it by the way she looks at you. She didn't even pay attention to other men when you are together.

Just like my Rowena." Robert is not even bothered that he is yelling. It's the reason why among the five of them Robert is the manager of the entire resort.

"Tsk, tsk." Yelling at this man won't work.

"So, what's going on?"

He didn't answer him but thinking if he can tell Robert about his and Casslynn's situation. He's staring at the empty space and gave a very loud sigh.

"Wooh, that was deep. What's wrong with our friend here, hmm?" Ben just came in with Maridelle, his fiancee.

"Sweetheart, can I get to the penthouse now?" He gave her the key of the main door to the penthouse.

"Sure. I'll see you later, Sweetheart. I love you."

He saw how Ben hug his fiancee. Maridelle is beautiful. But of course, Casslynn is even more beautiful.

Shit!

"Ehem! Let me guess, that is not the first time you curse this morning." Ben started talking. "So what's the problem, bro?"

"Do you really think I have a problem?" He asked sounded relaxed not sure if his face looks calmed or more problematic.

"Affirmative." Robert and Ben answered him in duet.

"Silly. I need to return some voicemails now." He doesn't want them to know.

"You know you cannot hide it from us. We are not friends for years now if we can't tell when you are having a very big problem or not." Said Ben.

"I don't think you can help."

"Try us." Robert tried to persuade him.

He walked towards the counter before he told them. "Casslynn is pregnant."

"What???" They asked him again in duet.

"Why did you get her pregnant?" Ben asked looking like there's a bomb planted inside the bar.

"When are you going to marry her?" Robert asked looking shocked.

"I didn't even know how I became so reckless, didn't think of using protection. It just happened. It wasn't planned. It's, it's a mistake."

"Stupid man. Don't say it's a mistake. It's a baby. A blessing. So when you do plan to hold the wedding?"

"Oh c'mon Rob, you know I am not the marrying type."

"And how you are you going to resolve this? I know Casslynn, she is not the kind of woman you used to date before. I know she would demand marriage." Robert is trying to convince him to marry her.

"I'm thinking of abortion."

Just then Ben grab his collar and give him a quick but strong punch on the face.

"You're so stupid! You know what if I would get Maridelle pregnant right now I will celebrate it with the world. You got a very nice woman pregnant and then killed the life she's carrying inside her? What kind of idiot are you?!?"

He got up and tried to hit him back when Robert grab his fist.

"Stop it, Alexis!"

"What right do you have to hit me on the face? You are just a friend! You are not father, not even my brother!" He shouted at Ben.

"Thank heavens we are not blood related. Because if we are, I will not only hit you on the face but I will going to kill you!"

Few people are in the bar and looking at them. Two big men fighting each other while Robert who's trying to be a middle man is also a big guy.

"Stop it, you two! Before I can even punch both of you, leave the bar now! And you Alexis, I need you to make up your mind. You cannot just ask Casslynn to abort the baby. Don't be an idiot! Or like Ben I might just want to kick you!"

He left the resort feeling so angry!

When he reached the condo, he opened a bottle of J.Walker and drink it all like water. He felt a little dizzy. But still he see the image of Casslynn being naked and smiling at him in his mind.

Shit!

He opened another bottle.

He's not going to marry Casslynn. But he also doesn't want to kill that baby inside her.

What am I going to do?

Chapter 25

IT'S been almost a month when she received a message from Alexis.

"Let's talk. I'll pick you up at LGP's."

She didn't even bother to reply. She doesn't understand why Alexis has to bother her again.

She's just sitting on one of the couch in the receiving area across the receptionist's area when one of the employees came in brought some plastics of food. Another employee open it and the smell of the food made her throw up. She hurriedly ran to the rest room.

She only vomits pure saliva.

She watched her face in the mirror. She looked pale and thin. She has not eaten in the past few days. Didn't even have proper sleep. She's starting to feel the effect of pregnancy in her body. She can't go through all these hardships alone after all she wasn't alone when this little life was created.

Argh!

How on earth can she asked Alexis to support her? Her pregnancy wasn't planned.

After a long period of staring in the mirror, staring at nothing, she decided to go home. She will try to get some rest tonight.

A man meet her at the reception area. She didn't expect to see him here.

"I thought you went home already. I was about to leave and go to your apartment."

"I couldn't believe you would come here."

"I sent you a message said I'd come here. We need to talk, I guess." His face is so serious. Looks like this man also didn't have much sleep. He has eye bugs. He showed some beard growing.

"I don't see why we need to talk." She started to walk towards the door.

"You know that we need to." He sounded like begging.

"If it's about the pregnancy-"

"We need to talk, Casslynn, but not here. I beg you. I'm really tired and sleepy. We need to get this over with. Let's go to Andromeda. I can still drive."

He is not calling her *ganda* anymore. Is she not beautiful to his eyes anymore?"

"I am not going anywhere with you, Alexis."

He stared at her. She looks pale and thin. But she's still very beautiful. Ah, must be the effect of pregnancy. He missed this woman terribly.

"Alright, I will sleep in your apartment then."

"You can't stay there." She still tried to fight with him.

"Don't be stubborn. I know pregnancy made you that. But I was telling the truth when I said I'm tired and sleepy."

Without a second, he carried her like a bride, straight to his car. He opened the passenger door with his feet. How he did it? She had no idea.

He drive 'til they reached her apartment.

He still carried her like she's something delicate.

"Put me down."

"Stop fighting, you'll get hurt."

He climb upstairs and put her on the bed.

"Why here? Did you even consider that I have not eaten anything yet?" She said. Though she doubt if she can swallow anything at this point.

He didn't answer her. She saw him dialing someone on his phone. Then she heard him giving his name and her apartment's address.

"Yes, anything that's good for a pregnant woman. But not something with garlic or could cause irritation on the nose. Don't have anything spicy. And include any unripe fruit or anything that's sour. No, no. Just that. And I need it here in less than 30 minutes!"

Then he heard him cursing.

"I am just going to make sure the car is parked well. Just stay on the bed. I ordered food for us."

Without waiting her to answer, he went outside. The next thing she heard was his car's engine. He must have moved the car in the garage. This apartment has garage though she doesn't have a car.

He came back inside. She was just looking at what he's doing. He came to her room again. Trying to adjust the AC's temperature.

"Is this good? Not too cold, not too hot?" He asked her.

"Yeah. It's the same temp as before, you don't need to adjust it."

"It's different now. Your body temperature changed because of pregnancy. How about the bed? Don't you think it's too soft? Do you want to put on some mat here?"

"It's fine. Why are you doing this, Alexis?"

"I just want to make you comfortable."

"You know that it's not what I mean."

"What do you want me to do?" He looked miserable. Well, that's how she see him. But she could be wrong. Why Alexis would be miserable? He should leave her alone. Dump her just like what he did to his previous women.

"We are supposed to talk about how to get rid of this. How do we go with abortion?"

For a minute, she saw a little flicker of anger in his eyes. But again she could be wrong. She no longer trust her judgment.

"We are not going to have abortion, Casslynn. I have too much sin already the hell can't take them all. If we need to keep it, we will."

'IT'. That's how he call the baby she's carrying inside her.

"This is not planned." She's expecting him to change his mind.

"True. But we both enjoyed the sex. You should not be going through all the troubles of pregnancy alone. I want to share my bargain. I will take care of you, at least while you're pregnant. But don't ask me marriage, I cannot give that to you."

That's going to be the next thing she would ask him.

Her heart almost break into pieces. She knows he would never marry her. She knows that from the beginning. She's about to burst into tears, thanks to the man who pressed the doorbell outside.

"I'll get it. It could be our order already."

While he went downstairs to get the food he ordered, she took the time to wipe the tears in the rest room.

There she let all the tears run down. Until there was nothing to flow. Nothing was left but anger. She's angry at herself why she allow her heart to fall for him. This is what she was scared before. She should not be meeting Alexis. She lost it again. Her heart. Her trust. But it's different now, she has a baby to take care of.

She heard a knock on the door. It was Alexis.

"*Ganda,* get out now. The food is ready."

He called her that again.

Okay.

If this is how it should be, then be it. If Alexis wants to take care of her while she's pregnant, fine. If he wants to father her baby, good. But she will never mentioned about love or marriage to him. They are together because of the baby, nothing else.

"I'm coming."

She made sure there's no sign of her crying. One last look of herself in the mirror and she know she's going to be fine.

She was surprised to see different kinds of food on the table.

"This is not for two people. We are not inviting your friends, are we?" Her eyes widened with disbelief.

"Three. We are now three. And no my friends are not coming."

"How do you think we can eat all these?" She asked. But starting to grab one of the delicious grapes on the platter.

"Just sit, *ganda*. I don't want you to get hungry. Eat all you want."

"You don't plan to make me match my size with McDonalds, do you?"

He laugh.

Oh, how she missed his laugh.

"Not really. But you're thin. And even if you will get fat you are still very beautiful, so I don't mind at all."

"Hmp!" She tried to scoop a spoon of soup. Then tastes the rest of the food served.

It seemed to be just five minutes. But the next moment she glanced at Alexis she saw him staring at her, smiling. When she looked at the plates again, almost each plate of food is half-empty.

"I'm hungry, I guess." She can't believe she take amount of food that's good for three people.

"I enjoyed watching you eating. Even while eating you are so sexy. You aroused me."

Oh, this pervert!

"Tell me you are not planning to have sex with me." She gave him a warning look.

"I was told it's even more enjoyable to make love to a pregnant woman. Most pregnant women, someone told me, are wild in bed."

"You're filthy."

"I'm not. I would love to enjoy your taste, especially down there. Our baby might want to witness his daddy exploring the feminine gate of her mommy's heaven."

She felt her face blushing. Not because this man is trying to seduce her but because of the way he said.

His daddy. Her mommy.

Creepy. But she's having a vision of twins.

God forbid.

"Why don't you enjoy the food and clean this afterward?"

"Oh my, this is what I fear." He said.

"What?"

"Robert, told me, that when Rowena was pregnant with their eldest child, Rowena made him a slave."

She just raised him an eyebrow.

"But I don't mind being your slave though."

"Well, then, hurry and finish your food." She glared at him.

"After you castrate me, though."

Her eyes widened again.

"Crazy."

"I mean it, Casslynn." He said seriously.

"Gross."

Chapter 26

SHE woke up in the middle of the night feeling horny. Alexis made love to her twice and the father of her baby slummed to sleep right after.

He snore loudly when he's tired and she knows that he is very tired now. She can't help but stare at his handsome face. Even when sleeping Alexis is like Adonis. Every woman will get tempted to peck a kiss on his luscious lips.

And she just pecked a kiss on him.

It was just a smack. But she was tempted to make the kiss even deeper. She tried to open his mouth. Even if his eyes are closed his mouth responded to her kisses.

"Kiss stealers are always punished." She heard him warning her, still with closed eyes.

"And how would you like to punish me? Mmmm." She ask him seductively while still kissing him.

He still didn't open his eyes.

"Mmmm, yummy kiss. How about you choose your punishment *ganda?*"

"I want you to beat me 'til I'm out of breath. Punch and slap me with your big cock 'til my eyes get blurry with pleasure. Prison me to the doors of heaven, yummy." Now she's really feeling wet.

"*Ganda,* don't you feel tired?" He doesn't sound like he's gonna fall to her seduction. But she saw how his perfectly, beautiful male member hardened.

"Are you sure you want me to sleep? I can see that your big gun is rising up so strong. What a fighter!"

She grab his manhood with her bare hand.

"*G-ganda,* stop it."

"I won't Alexis. I'm feeling horny, yummy. I can't sleep." Now she's sitting on top of him, right there with his bulgy manhood.

Now, she's trying to push his big bleep inside her.

"Ah, shit, this is great, Alexis. I love it when you are very hard."

"Oh, Casslynn, the pregnancy has a bad effect on you. You are becoming horny and this is just your 2nd month."

"Are you complaining, huh? Ahh." She moves faster on top of him.

"Not really. But you are draining all my energy. Ohh." She could feel his orgasm.

"Oh, please, don't tell me you are going to cum so fast now. Oh no. I have not had enough yet."

She can sense he is trying to stop from cumming.

"I am not going to disappoint you pretty preggy. Now, let me do the work." In just a second he had her lay down. Now he is on top of her. "I'm still scared I will crush you and the baby."

"Trust me, you won't. Now, please push faster, yummy."

"Your wish is my command my queen."

She felt him pushing faster and deeper. She's running out of breath but she can't help scream his name.

And next thing, she felt the warmth seed bursting inside her.

"Do you think your sperm can make another baby inside making them two?"

"Silly."

"What do you think is our baby? Is he going to be a boy? Or will she be a girl?"

"Either boy or girl, its fine." He started to close his eyes.

"Are you really sure you want me to stay here?" Two days ago she decided to accept his invitation of having her stay in his condo.

"I am *ganda*." His voice started to lower.

"Are you sure you want to father my baby?" She's looking at his face while talking. Alexis is really handsome.

"Yes."

"Are you sure you won't fall in love with me?"

His answer is simply a snore.

"I'm sorry for making you so tired." She sleep on top of him. She love his scent so much. He smells like cherry. His tempting fragrance made her fall asleep so easily.

But two hours later she woke up feeling horny again. But she saw Alexis sleeping so peacefully. She slide to his side and rest in his arm.

She tried to close her eyes again but she's really feeling horny. They are both naked. But Alexis's big bird is asleep just like him.

Shit!

What am I going to do now?

She tried to kiss him again, but Alexis responded with a snore. She grab his hand and tried to put in on her breast.

"*Ganda*...sleep." She heard him murmuring.

"I can't. I'm feeling horny again. Can you fuck me once more?"

She knows he is very sleepy but he tried his best to open an eye.

"Hmmm. Ah pregnancy cravings. *Ganda*...come and sit on my top. And push. He is already up."

True. His enormous male is now up.

"Oh yeah, I love this."

Then she push his male organ inside her and pump. The feeling is heavenly.

It took him few minutes only and Alexis explode again.

"There. I hope you can sleep now." He gave her deep and sweet kiss. "Goodnight, beautiful."

"Thank you." She kissed him goodnight.

And truly she fell asleep 'til morning.

Chapter 27

"HA HA. That's so funny, bro."

He is working in the bar today. The first thing his friends noticed when he came in was his look. He told them how he got those black circles around his eyes.

"Don't laugh at me, Franky. You have no idea how difficult it is to sleep with a horny, pregnant woman."

All four of them laugh. But Robert is the one who's laughing so loud.

"One of the things that men should sacrifice. You know, to give in to all the pregnant woman's cravings. It's great that Casslynn craves on sex." He can see his friend laughing with tears now.

"Tsk, tsk. Trust me it's not great, Rob. Every now and then Casslynn woke up feeling horny." Casslynn is almost four-month pregnant now.

"How I wish when I married Maridelle and she got pregnant she would crave on sex. I swear I wouldn't even hesitate a second to have sex with her." Ben said.

"Don't wish for it, bro. I always feel fully-drained every time she wake me up for sex."

"That's weird. Before you met Casslynn you cannot live a day without sex, bro." Charlie said.

"It's different now. Casslynn is asking for it like four or five times in a night, not to mention in the morning before I left for work and when I come home from work. Honestly, there are times I want to shout at her, but I just can't."

"Oops, don't you ever shout at a pregnant woman, nor hurt her. It's affecting the baby, bro." Robert warned him.

"Who knows it's going to be a boy and will grow up as Casanova."

He cussed. Never will he allow his son to become like him. It's never good to be a womanizer.

"Stop it, Charlie. I won't let that happen."

"Oh? How did your father stop you from becoming a womanizer? I think your father failed to do that either."

"I actually want to ask your help and advice. But guys you are making me feel even more miserable. I don't know what to do with, Casslynn."

"Speaking of Casslynn, bro. She's on the phone. Wants to talk to you. Warned me to give the phone to you or she will come here and explode this place." Ben chuckled.

"She can't do that." He looked at him annoyed while going to where the telephone rack is placed.

"I didn't know Casslynn is a tigress when she's pregnant." Robert laugh.

He just gave them dirty finger. And they all laugh at him.

"Hello, *ganda*." He started to talk to her. He is hearing a music in the background. "*Ganda* what was that?" He asked her, now having suspicion of what the music is.

"It's a music, yummy. Careless Whisper."

"Holy mother! Why are you playing that song? It's for-" He wasn't able to finish speaking.

"I'm feeling horny. Can you buy me a dildo so when you are not around I can play with myself?"

Holy mother of earth!

What will he do to this woman?

"Yummy, are you there?"

"Y-yes. I'm here." He is having a real bad headache.

"Can you buy me one when you get home? I want the expensive one, 6-inch fake dick, please?" He can guess she's pouting.

"Do you really need that? I mean, we can have sex when I get home." He doesn't want to buy her one.

"Did you hear me say, 'I will do it when you are not home', okay? Please, yummy?"

"I can't promise."

"Well, you need to promise me."

"What if I can't?"

"Well, you will not sleep beside me."

Now that's something he cannot allow to happen. Not only that Casslynn wakes up at night feeling horny, but she's also hungry and eats anything that came to her mind.

"Okay, I will buy you one."

"Two. Make it two."

"Crap."

"Are you cursing, Alexis?" She sounded mad. Robert is right. Casslynn turned into a tigress because of pregnancy.

"Not really, *ganda*."

"Alright. Go back to work now. I don't want Robert to think that I'm abusing his kindness."

"I will see you later, *ganda*."

Chapter 28

THE last month of the first trimester of Casslynn's pregnancy was terrible.

There was no time that Casslynn is not horny. Even after five rounds, Casslynn was still horny and the dildo he bought for her really did a great job.

But when she reached the first month of the second trimester, Casslynn's attitude change. It's like the north switched to south. From being horny she turned into someone who doesn't even want a kiss. There are few nights that Casslynn didn't want to sleep with him. He was forced to sleep outside his own bedroom a couple of times. There were couple of instances that he was not even allowed to enter his own house.

When she reached the last trimester of her pregnancy. Her attitude and cravings changed, too.

Casslynn turns into a very romantic woman.

She always wait for him and greet him with a kiss. Just like now, he saw her sitting on the couch with her bulgy stomach while reading a magazine.

"Hey, pretty."

When she saw him, she smiled sweetly at him. Rose up from her seat and throw him a hug.

"Hi, yummy. How are you? Hmm, you are so sweaty." Then she gave him a deep kiss. "I prepared your house wear. Hold on let me get it for you." He saw her walking upstairs, to their bedroom.

He can't help but smiled. The past few months had been like a rollercoaster for him. But eventually, everything seems to be fine. Casslynn is getting more and more beautiful every day, one thing that seems to be weird. From what he knows pregnant women usually turned ugly as their stomach grow bigger, but Casslynn isn't. Even at her 6th month where she looks like 8-month pregnant she's very pretty. Another thing that made it weird because Casslynn's stomach seemed to be in enormous size. It isn't normal. But when he asked her how she feels, she said she feels good.

"Sorry for taking so long. Here are your clothes. Now get changed and I'm hungry, yummy. Follow me to the kitchen."

Oh he forgot there's another thing that didn't change. Casslynn still sounds like his boss. But he didn't mind. She's a damn, sexy boss.

He followed her into the kitchen.

Another thing he didn't mention is that Casslynn is a good cook.

"What do we have for today?"

"Grilled pork. Chopsuey. Sautéed mushroom and seashells and we have the fried fish fillet." She said while handing him his plate.

"This is awesome. I am so hungry."

"Taste it first."

He did.

"Yummy."

"Don't use that term."

"Why?"

"The food is delicious. You are yummy." Then she smiled at him again.

"Oh, *ganda*. Didn't I remind you not to smile at me that way?"

"We are eating, yummy. Don't get too much engrossed with sex. Now eat."

Sometimes he wish Casslynn gets horny again. But himself is not into too much sex anymore either. Well, they seldom have sex. It was his choice. He doesn't want to hurt her and the baby. So he's always doing DIY (Do-It-Yourself).

While eating they talk about all things.

She asked him about his job at the resort. Or how the resort is going. She praised him for doing a good job in getting more reservations. But when he told her about a flirt girl, she pinched him.

"Ouch, *ganda*. That hurts! How can I swallow my food now?"

"Don't be silly, Alexis. It's just a pinch on your arm. Do you want me to pinch your balls?"

"Oh my. Would love that. Can you cut them into half?"

She laughed at him. Oh how he love the laughter of this woman.

"I know you would say that. You still not over with your obsession of getting castrated, right?"

"Not until you do it."

"I won't."

"I bet you will one day."

They both laugh together.

It took them more than an hour to finish dinner. They ended up bursting another laughter when he told her how he told his friends about her obsession on sex during the first trimester of her pregnancy.

"Are you not mad at me?"

"Of course not. I am glad you told them. It sounded like you are a sex slave."

"Crazy. Now I will wash all these dishes and you wait for me in the living room, okay?"

"I will go prepare our bedroom and wait for you afterwards."

"My kiss first?"

She gave him a quick peck on the lips.

"You taste more delicious than the grilled pork."

And she gave him another laughter that made him smile.

Chapter 29

THE next three months had been busy months for both him and Casslynn.

Casslynn is still writing romance books even though she is not comfortable sitting with big tummy.

And he was busy trying to plan what to do with the baby. He won't deny that he felt a little excitement that soon his little angel would appear in this wild world.

Neither he nor Casslynn knows the gender of the baby yet. They didn't choose to undergo an ultrasound as they want to be surprised.

Casslynn is having trouble moving inside the house due to her big stomach.

Sometimes she woke up at night feeling like she wants to piss. Or sometimes very hungry. Sometimes she woke up feeling horny. It's like everything that happened in the past months was combined into one.

"Alexis, where is my dildo here?"

And yes, he bought her another dildo when she demanded to have one a week ago.

"*Ganda,* I didn't use it. You go look for it."

"It's not here. Help me look for it. Now!" She's shouting right from the bathroom.

And sometimes she's too demanding, shouting at him every minute.

"Can you get out? I will look for it."

He shut down his laptop and started to look for the dildo inside their bedroom. He seemed to be looking for it like forever when he heard her shouting again from the bathroom.

"Oh, it's here! Just inside the toothbrush rack. Never mind!"

Grrr!

When this is over, swear to heaven he will not touch Casslynn again. He will never get her pregnant again. Ah, he's almost running out of patient for this woman.

He checked on her and found that she's playing with her vagina using the dildo.

"What do you think you are doing?" He grab the dildo from her hand.

"Give me that!" She protest.

"No, you're hurting our baby."

"Then fuck me! I feel so horny."

"Shit, Casslynn, your tummy is even bigger than a two basketballs and you still want sex! My goodness!"

"Then give me back my fake dick!" She's shouting again. He can see how her nerves are becoming visible in her neck.

Shit!

He silently cursed. He doesn't want to get her upset.

"Alright. Come here." He carried her and help her fixed on the bed. "If it's sex. I can do it gently. Now, spread your legs."

She greatly obeyed.

Just then he realized how he is having a strong hard on.

He pushed his male organ inside her. He can see how her eyes glowed with pleasure.

"Yeahh. I like that, yummy. Please go on. Kiss me." He kissed her. "Faster, Alexis!" She's shouting her name.

"Oh baby. I like it when you scream my name." He dig deeper and faster as she commanded.

He exploded inside her.

"Oh, that was heaven! Yummy, you never failed to pleasure me."

"And you always made me a satisfied man. But I still don't get enough of you. Wait, 'til our baby is out. You are going to pay for all the shouting and unreasonable demand you've made."

"Oh my, I am excited to make the payment, yummy."

Shit!

He cursed again. Didn't he promise earlier that he will not touch her again?

Just then the phone rang.

Casslynn is closer to the phone rack.

"Hey, Cass, we are on our way to Alexis' condo. We are bringing some food. We'll be there in 5 minutes or so." It was Shane.

"What? Who's with you?" She panicked. Five minutes and she's lying naked with legs spread and Alexis is still having a hard on.

"Who is that?" Alexis asked when he saw the panic in her face.

"It's the entire team, Cass. I will hung up now. I will see you in few minutes."

"It's Shane. My team will be here in less than five minutes!"

"What?" Now it's Alexis who panicked.

"Yes! Now, get off me and put on your clothes! It will take me few minutes to get dressed, so you go downstairs and open the door for them."

"What? I'm still hard. Do you have any idea how my big birdie would stick up outside my shorts?" It's true, Alexis had an enormous penis that if he's having a hard on it would make his shorts look like it's making a three-story tent.

"Well then, wear a thick pants. Now, go and do as I told you!"

"Shit!"

He hurriedly chose one pants from the dresser and a T-shirt, while she's still on the bed lying naked.

"Is this okay? How do you see my big birdie from outside?"

"Not too obvious. Now, help me get up, my stomach is very heavy."

He held him up and peck a kiss on her lips.

"Do you want me to help you get dressed?" He asked seductively.

"Silly. No! And don't use that tone on me or no one will open the door."

"Ha ha. Alright. I will go downstairs now. Looks like our visitors are here." He gave him another kiss before he ran the stairs.

Alexis saw nine beautiful women waiting outside. But none of them could match the beauty of Casslynn.

"Hello ladies. I am glad to see all of you. Get inside."

"Hi, handsome. Where's Casslynn?" It was Victoria he guess. Until now he is still having hard time identifying Casslynn's friends. He is not really good with names.

He guide the women inside and called Casslynn.

"Wow, these are Casslynn's favorite. Thank you for this, Em." He said to Emily Higgins.

"Don't mention it, Alexis. I am glad that you are taking care of Casslynn. I thought you would just leave her after getting her pregnant." Em said seriously.

"Oh, there she is." They heard the curly woman talk. He guessed the name is Brenn or was that Shen?

"Hello, ladies. Thanks for coming. Did you bring me something?" Casslynn slowly walked and gave each lady a hug.

"Of course. We know your cravings, so we had them on the table." Shane said.

"Your stomach is growing so big, Cass. When is your due date?" Em asked and sounded worried.

"I still have two weeks, Em."

"Looks like you are about to deliver him out."

Him.

That's how her friends address the baby in her womb. She doesn't really have any idea of the baby's gender.

"Not yet, Jenna." She said while laughing at them. "Oh, where's the food. Can I take a look?"

"Are you sure you just want to look at it?" Adelaide joked.

"Silly. Of course not. But I have no plan to share it with you."

"Now that's unfair."

Everyone laugh.

Alexis guided her through the table. While Carly asked to play some music. They were enjoying the food. While the other ladies are dancing to the music.

"Let me get to the bathroom." She said. She felt like wanting to piss again. She's been like this since last night.

"Let me go with you." Alexis said. He looked more worried now.

"No. Stay with them." She said and rushed to the bathroom.

It only took about a minute when Alexis heard her shouting from the bathroom.

Everyone paused and automatically ran to the bathroom.

There they saw liquids flowing in between Casslynn's thighs.

"I think she's about to deliver her child."

Alexis went pale.

Chapter 30

"CAN you at least take a seat? You are like a dog that cannot piss, bro." Ben said irritably.

Two hours ago he called his friends and told them Casslynn is going to deliver the baby. All four of them except Franky who was left in the resort watching the counter rushed to the hospital right away.

"Just please relax, Alexis, Casslynn will be fine." Shane told him.

"Let him Shane. You know a big man who pretend to be brave but when his wife is delivering his baby got scared? That's normal for big men." Victoria tried to tease him.

"Tsk! You are not helping."

He admit it, he got scared. Casslynn is a small woman and he has no idea how big is the baby inside her. Judging by the size of her belly it looks like the baby is big. Well, it's partly his fault because he just let Casslynn ate anything she wanted during the entire pregnancy period.

"I know how you feel, bro. Been there when Rowena gave birth to our first child. I could still feel the power of fear of possibly losing her and the guilt of having her go through all the pain when I got her pregnant. But one lesson I learned, you should not be surrounded with women while waiting for hours for her to bring your child in this world." Robert told him after forcing a wicked smile.

"And just what do you mean by that?" Adelaide glare at Robert.

Robert just gave out a laugh.

He didn't pay attention to them. He is really scared.

"What time is it now?" He asked Em.

"It's not three hours yet since Casslynn gone to the delivery room." Em answered him.

"What? Not three hours yet? What's taking it so long?" He stand and about to go to the delivery room when five women stopped him.

"Husbands are not allowed in the delivery room." Brenn said.

"Not even female friends." Carly added.

"And just to remind you, Casslynn is delivering a baby, not a puppy." Jenna sounded like she wants to strangle him.

"When I deliver my first baby, it took me 10 hours to stay inside the delivery room." Freda just simply smiled.

"Ten hours? Oh my goodness!" He can't believe these women are telling him to wait for more hours to see Casslynn.

"Do you really make it a habit to repeat people's words?" Victoria turned from teasing him to getting pissed at him.

"Why don't we ladies go out and buy some food? It's going to be a long night." Em said and walk away without waiting for the other ladies to answer. The rest of the women from LGP followed Em.

He was left with Robert, Ben and Charlie.

"I would agree with the women bro, you should get relaxed." Charlie told him.

"How the hell am I going to get relaxed when I know that Casslynn is inside that room for hours now? And what? I am going to wait another hours! This is driving me insane." He felt upset. Frustrated. Scared. Worried. And all the negative emotions in the world.

Robert and Ben just laughed at him.

"Swear to heavens, I am not going to get her pregnant again."

This time Robert's laugh grow louder.

"Why the hell are you laughing with me?"

"I could see myself. You know that it's the same words I said when Rowena delivered our first child. Same words I had when she gave birth to the second. Now, she is pregnant again. And I know that same exact words will come out from my mouth again when the big day comes." Robert simply told him.

"That was you. I'm a different person. Trust me. This will be Casslynn's last pregnancy." He said with firm conviction.

"Should be, bro. Otherwise, learn to get shame of not marrying her yet making her pregnant. On her next pregnancy you should be marrying her already." Ben seriously said.

"Tsk, tsk. There you go again. I told you that my relationship with Casslynn is just a father to her kid. I am not even her boyfriend, so much of marrying her."

"You're saying that you really have no plan to marry her?" Charlie asked him in disbelief.

"You know that I am not a marrying type. No woman can ever tie me in marriage. I didn't even dream of a kid and this woman accidentally got pregnant so I have no choice."

"I don't know why you ever became my friend." Robert said.

"Stop pushing me guys. It's not helping in this situation." He simply said while still glancing at the delivery room from time to time.

"We are helping you to make up your mind. Casslynn is a treasure, bro." Ben said.

"Maridelle just might want to hear you said that." He threatened him.

"Silly, Maridelle is not the jealous type."

"I will make her."

"You are crazy, Alexis."

He didn't answer. Why did he feel a little pain inside? Surely his friends don't have special desire for Casslynn, he hopes. Casslynn is his.

Shit!

Can't believe he felt jealous of his friends admiring Casslynn.

*****

Few hours later, Casslynn's friends arrive. They brought box of pizzas and canned drinks.

"Here. We bought you guys food and drinks." Em said. She pass the pizza box and drinks to Robert.

They ate what the women brought for them.

Other women were busy checking their phones. While Emily Higgins was checking something in her laptop. Even in the hospital these ladies are bringing their works with them.

Tsk, tsk.

He silently prayed inside. For the first time he learned to pray. He doesn't have any idea how long they have stayed waiting outside the delivery room. Five hours? Six hours? It could be longer than that. He didn't take any glance at his watch, afraid that the time will stop the next time he look.

"This is not good. Are you sure it's normal for a woman to deliver a child for more than 10 hours now? Rowena delivered our first child after 8 hours." Robert said. You can hear a little panic in his voice.

No one answered him. But an excited Franky arrives.

"Hey, bro. What's Casslynn's baby?"

Few hours ago, Ben and Charlie left to go to the resort.

"She's still inside the delivery room." Shane told him.

"Oh, fuck. Why it's taking so long? I thought you brought her here late morning today." He look at his watch. "It's almost 8 in the evening." He counted. "Fuck, eleven hours?" They arrive in the hospital nine in the morning.

"Wait, I think the doctor is coming." Victoria said.

Everyone stand. Nervously waiting for the doctor to speak a word.

Alexis stood like a statue. Can't move. Can't speak. Didn't even blink.

"Who's the husband?" The doctor asked.

Alexis raised his hand.

Everyone looked at him, raising their eyebrows.

"Alright. I am not the husband. We are not married." He told everyone. "But I am the father of the baby."

The doctor smiled.

"Congratulations!" The doctor tapped his shoulder. "You are an amazing man!"

"Is it a boy?" He nervously asked.

"Is it a girl?" The women chorused.

"It's both." The doctor simply said.

"What do you mean?" Alexis asked, confused.

"Your wife gave birth to twins. A boy and a girl." The doctor said before turning away.

Alexis faint.

Chapter 31

"**W**HAT?"

It's been almost two months since they got home. The twins joyfully settled in their new home.

Yes, home. Finally there's a perfect word for the place he lives in. He loves to listen to the cry of babies inside the house that even when you are downstairs, in the kitchen or garage, the cries are heard.

And every time he looked at the twins peacefully sleeping he always remember how proud he is for having Casslynn as their mother.

Like right now, the twins are awake and he is just staring at Casslynn.

"You know that I don't like to be stared at."

"I am just proud to have you as mother of Lexa and Lex."

The twins are named Alexa Cassie and Lexand Casseus. Casslynn named the twins in the hospital. Another thing he is very proud of her. She made those lovely names in just a matter of seconds.

"You should be Mr. Andrews. The twins are both handsome and pretty. Too bad they look like your duplicate copy not mine." She teased him.

"You're saying they should look like you?" He teased her back.

"Why? What's the problem if the children would look like me?"

"I don't like them petite looking and short like you."

She glared at him.

"Asshole. If that's the case, then go look for tall women and stop fucking me!"

He just laugh at her. But hug her from the back while she's busy breastfeeding Alexa.

"I'm just teasing you, *ganda*. You know how I love your looks. You are my weakness. Your smile and lovely legs, they made me crazy." He said while starting to kiss the side of her mouth.

"I still don't give you the authority to kiss me. What you are doing is stealing. Stealing of kisses."

That's not really true. A month after she gave birth to the twins not only that he kissed her but he also started to make love to her again. And Casslynn as yummy as she was before she was pregnant became even yummier after she gave birth to the twins.

She smiled at him.

As expected, his mouth cursed. Why not, this woman always make him hard every time she smiles.

"And I don't need to remind you what that smile can do to me."

"Well, Alexa and Lexand wouldn't allow you, that's why they are not asleep yet. And Alexa is very hungry. Look."

True. Her princess is sucking her mother's nipple hungrily.

"It's not making me happy now that I have rivals in sucking your boobs, *ganda*."

Casslynn laugh.

"What are you doing?"

"Very good." He smiled after Casslynn stopped from laughing.

He carried Lexand in one arm. Kissed the forehead of Alexa. Then his other hand begin its busy work. He move his hand inside Casslynn's dress and found her cherry.

"Shit! Alexis, I'm feeding your girl." He can hear her moan a little while he is trying to finger fuck her. She's wet and how he wish his twins are asleep so he can lick and suck their mother.

"It's okay, *ganda*. They wouldn't know what I am doing. And don't worry as soon as they fall asleep my big gun then would already be fully hard and we will go to heaven together."

"Oh, Alexis. You are making me wet." He thrusts two fingers now and faster.

"I know. How I wish they would get sleep soon coz I am excited to taste your wet cherry pop, *ganda*."

Chapter 32

"SALUTE to JEWELS!!!"

This is what welcomed them when they arrive the expensive pavilion.

She's carrying Lexand in her arms while Alexis carried Alexa in his arms with big backpack in his back.

It's awarding day. As expected the JEWELS imprint led by Emily Higgins got four books featured in the All-Time Collection imprint of LGP. Once more her book and with Brenn's, as well as Shane and Victoria's will be displayed in bookstores nationwide and the entire publishing is expecting it to be out of print in less than a month.

But that's not really the reason why she attended this celebration. She's not at all a party-goer. She's also not the kind to show off her success. Sure her books hit in the market, but that should be kept secret.

"Well, I should mention that one of the reasons behind our success are the pretty and handsome angels carried by those two lovely parents." Em's gave her speech and mentioned hers and Alexis' names.

A loud clap is heard in the background.

She silenced Em to finish her speech and it's important for her to talk to her.

"*Ganda* I am going to get you a drink." Alexis said leaving her on the seat.

Few minutes later, Em approached her on the table. With her is a guy and a beautiful girl.

"The answer is no, Casslynn." She told her even before she could ask her.

"But Em, this is a one-time offer. I wanted to feel the experience of writing a book for someone other than LGP. Just two books Em." She begged.

A month ago she received an offer to publish her book in a self-publishing company. The package is very expensive but Alexis is willing to spend money for her.

"I really wanted her to try it, Em. She has the talent. Writing a book for a company with policies too different than LGP that's a good thing." Alexis came with a glass of red liquid in his hand she believe is an Apple-Cherry juice.

"And I am going to use a different pen name, Em. Trust me."

"I discussed this with the rest of the team and they don't want you to do it." Em still refused.

"I am willing to bargain with you, Em."

"You have pending projects. I cannot afford to have you stop writing for LGP. How do you suppose to do it while working for this company?"

"She can do it." Alexis said.

"Alright. I will allow you to do it but in one condition." Em is now staring at her like she's asked to make a choice between life and death. Then she started to introduce the guy named Kenne Jay which she found out was a gay and the girl is Sadie Bryce. "They are new hires. They will accompany you to Frankfurt."

"Hello, Ms. Monica. I'm really happy to finally meet you. Oh sexylicious I didn't know you are still very young and beautiful. I guess I am destined to be your companion based on beauty." Kenne Jay said.

"Yuck. Did you hear yourself? Do you want me to get you a mirror?" Sadie Bryce raised an eyebrow to the gay before facing her. "Oh hi, Ms. Monica. I'm an avid fan. It's my joy to really see you in person. And don't believe that gay, if this a fairytale you will be Snow White and I am Rapunzel, and that gay is the ugly, evil witch."

She laughed with these two. Before she glanced back at Em. "I know and I accepted it. But I will bring Alexis and the twins with me, Em."

"Are you sure they won't bother you?" Em asked with suspicion.

Alexis chuckled.

"I will take care of the twins while she's busy working, Em."

"Alright, that's settled now. The car is waiting for you outside. You could leave now or wait 'til the party is over."

"I am not much of a party pip so we'd rather leave now and my twins are getting upset with this noise."

Em just laugh.

She kissed the twins and told them to leave.

"Hey." She called Alexis. "For goodness sake, don't get her pregnant again." With awful voice tone. "And Sadie Bryce, Kenne Jay, you are with Casslynn to work not as tourists." She reminded the two new hired writers.

"Yes, momma." Sadie and Kenne said in duet.

"She's safe. She's breastfeeding, Em." Alexis told her smiling.

"Let's go." She dragged him before Em could say something else.

"She's a tigress." Alexis complained.

"A bit. But I like Em. She's like a mother to me."

They will go out of the country for a special job Em have for her.

Chapter 33

SHE felt exhausted when she reached come. She just came home from the city trying to argue with Em again about going back to Frankfurt.

Yes, a month ago she was in Frankfurt with Alexis and the twins. The new hires, Sadie Bryce and Kenne Jay were really good companions.

One of the books she wrote will be adapted into a movie by a French company and the signing of contract was held in Frankfurt. It's not just contract signing but she had to meet few people from the movie industry and needed to introduce herself as Monica. It's pretty tiring. While in the middle of agreement discussion she almost fell asleep and she's very sleepy. They stayed in Frankfurt for two weeks and she didn't like the foreign atmosphere.

She saw Alexis on the bed sleeping. Lexand is sleeping peacefully on his left, Alexa is smiling while sleeping on his right.

She felt a little pride looking at a big man like Alexis sleeping with little babies next to him.

She pecked a kiss on his lips.

She lie down next to Lexand and her eyelids closed in a matter of seconds.

But few hours later she woke up with the feeling that something is moving in between her thighs.

When she open her eyes she saw Alexis doing a mouth to mouth kiss with her cherry.

"Fuck, Alexis, what are you doing?" She was shouting but made a short stop after seeing the twins peacefully sleeping on the bed. She is lying down on the couch.

"Tasting your cherry, *ganda*. It's been few days since I last tasted you here. I really love sipping your juices."

"Don't. Oh, please." Instead of protest she heard herself moaning.

"I won't. Promise. I will make you happy, *ganda*." Then he continued licking her while thrusting one finger inside.

"H-how did I get here? I was sleeping on the bed with the twins. Ahh." She asked but still moaning a little.

"I moved you out from the bed. I can't afford to have the twins witnessed how I make love to their mother."

He moved from sucking her cherry to kissing her neck moving to her breasts and then to her stomach. He come to her waist area, move to one leg. Kissing her right inner thigh, then to her left. Teasing ever so slightly.

He is the master sucker if there's such a term. He's the God of Kissing and Licking.

She can't help but grab his hair and pull him closer to her cherry. Why can't this guy just go back straight to 'her' again?

He just keep teasing her, barely touching with one finger. She felt his finger and it's driving her crazy.

She almost jumped with so much need when he use his tongue and kiss so close to her cherry. He lick 'her' lips and that made her moan and wanting more. He lick her clit, playing around with it with his tongue slightly. Then use his tongue to lick right between the lips from the bottom up to her clit. Moving his tongue from side to side and in a circular motion. His tongue played with her clit as he take his finger and played with 'her' lips and then slowly go inside, making her eyes roll and giving out a moan. Her moan gets louder and louder and she felt her body moving and grabbing his hair. His fingers hit the right perfect spot and he played with her gspot. He take his fingers out and use his tongue, inserting in and out.

He get her on the edge of the couch, on her knees. As she bent over, her face is close to the couch.

"Alexis, please."

He teased her with his big gun from behind, then slowly put the head in and push deep inside her.

"Oh myy." She moaned again, this time it's louder.

"Let me hold you." He hold her shoulders and with the other hand her hair so she won't have her face on the couch.

It starts off with a slow penetration. And gets faster and faster. She could feel Alexis grasping for air.

Then he moved her to a different position. With legs spread wide, he inserted his big gun again, facing her. He is pushing so deep while staring at her face.

"Lovely." He is referring to her face. "The biggest reason why my twins are pretty and handsome."

She can't speak a word, she's grasping for air this time.

"My orgasm is getting me there. I can feel it, Alexis."

"Hold on, *ganda*. I can feel your wetness and your juices. We will get there together."

She can feel her legs start to come closer. And she can't help but grab his hair even more. She can hear their moans getting louder and louder. Breathing gets heavier and heavier. And they give one last moan together before his body starts to shake and the rush comes to his head from cumming. And she can feel her cumming, too, meeting with his.

He rested on her top.

"That was great, yummy." She exclaimed with joy and contentment.

"You are awesome, *ganda*. Did I make you happy?" He asked her, smiling.

"Happiest." She return his smile. And it's a surprise he didn't get hard. He just smiled at her again. And they are exchanging smiles, sign of complete satisfaction.

"I'm hungry." He told her.

"And you are still on my top. Can you do something?" She keeps smiling at him.

"Oh." He helped her get up. "Let's take shower together."

"Hmm. Another round under the shower?" She teased him.

"Hmm. Why not. I hope I didn't make you sore yet."

"Not yet. I can still take few more rounds." He then carried her to the shower room. "Put me down."

"Not until we are both under the flowing water."

And as expected they had another intense round under the shower. Was about to have the third round when they heard Lexand's cry.

"I guess my son won't let me have the third round." They both laugh.

Few seconds later, Alexa wake up, too.

They decided to bring the twins downstairs to see the sunrise. There's a table with two benches close to the fountain outside the house and a swing.

"*Ganda,* I am going to get some snack inside. Stay here." He left her with the twins on the swing.

He came back carrying a plate of fries. The first thing that caught her is the bad smell of the fries.

"What's that? Argh, take that away. The smell is awful!"

"This is your favorite. Remember you bought couple of this from last month? I just realized we still have few packs inside the fridge."

"No, take that away, please."

But before he can go back inside the house to return the fries, she throw up. She had not eaten anything since four hours ago and now she had thrown away what was left inside her stomach.

Alexis stared at her with shock.

"No, you can't be-"

"What? I told you to throw that fries away. I don't like the smell of it." She didn't pay attention to him again. She was just staring at the twins. They are three months old now.

"When was your last menstruation?" Alexis asked her still with shocking look.

"Two months ago or so. I'm not sure. Since I live with you I never care about my period anymore. I don't have time to monitor my-" A sudden realization also shock her. She vomit. She hated the smell of garlic. She easily gets worn out, she's having the same attitude again. "No, no. You are not thinking I am pregnant, are you?" It scared her. Not again. Please.

She saw him throwing punch in the air.

"Cannot be. But oh, goodness. The twins are only three months old."

"I cannot get pregnant again. No. What are we going to do now?" She panic.

"Let me buy a pregnancy test device. Or let's go to the doctor to be sure."

"Bullshit! That's not my question, Alexis."

"Bullshit, too, Casslynn. I don't know!"

The twins cried.

Chapter 34

ROBERT was laughing at him after he told him the news.

"What's up? Why this married is man laughing to the bones?" Franky just arrived with Ben and Charlie.

"You won't believe it brothers." Robert almost roll on the floor laughing.

"Tsk, tsk. I didn't tell you just to laugh at me. I need help." He looked at his other three friends. Maybe they can help him. "Casslynn is pregnant again."

"What? Ha ha." Just like Robert, Ben laugh at him, too. So does Charlie and Franky.

He feels even more miserable. How can his friends laugh at him at situation like this?

"I don't know why I call you friends." He grab one glass of wine.

"C'mon bro. No kidding. How old are the twins? Three months? And Casslynn is pregnant again? Amazing!" Ben said with surprising look.

"My goodness! You are one hell of a sharp shooter bro." Franky said with amazement.

"You bet. My eldest was almost two years when Rowena was pregnant with our second child." Robert said.

"Have you not heard of family planning, bro?" Charlie asked him.

"Casslynn was breastfeeding. I didn't expect her to get pregnant this early." He said, still feeling miserable.

"Some women easily get pregnant when they are fertile bro, and breastfeeding sometimes fail to do its job." Charlie told him.

"How do you know, Charlie?" Franky ask, looking at Charlie suspiciously.

"Silly. I didn't get any woman pregnant yet, I just know."

"So, now that she's pregnant again, when do you plan to marry her? You cannot just have Casslynn raise and deliver your babies without commitment, bro." Robert said seriously.

"That's the biggest problem. I cannot marry her. And I want to get rid of the baby she's carrying now. Two is too much. I cannot afford to have the third." Next thing he heard is a big thing hitting his face. Robert's fist.

"Don't show me your face until you're back to your senses, asshole!" Robert left furiously.

Chapter 35

"YOU are stupid, Casslynn! Stupid!"

Emily Higgins is very mad. Shouting at her and calling her names.

"Enough, Em. Don't get the pregnant woman upset." Shane tried to calm their editor who is now beyond furious.

"Call me when this idiot had make up her mind. I hate to slap her beautiful face!" Em left them.

She can't help but cry. She hates it when Em is angry.

"How did it happen?" Jenna asked her.

"Another idiot!" Victoria look mad but she can see that she's doing her best to help her. "Of course, she and Alexis had sex that's why she's pregnant AGAIN."

"I thought you were on breastfeeding?" Adelaide asked, looking at her with pity.

"I was."

She's at LGP now. She told her team that she's pregnant again. She thought the women would be happy for her but it's the opposite. Em walked out filled with anger. She reminded her before not to get pregnant again.

"You were? What do you mean?" Brenn asked.

"When we were at Frankfurt and I was busy meeting with the movie staff I had to leave the twins with Alexis and he bottle-feed them of course."

"Holy shit! That was it. You were not careful. You should not have sex with him after-"

"You know that I cannot resist Alexis' charms, Victoria."

"Let's stop blaming, Casslynn. Let's help her." Carly said. Finally, someone is trying to offer a hand.

"How the hell can we help you?" It was still Victoria.

"That is not the question!" Adelaide glared at her. "Maybe this time that asshole Alexis do have the plan to marry you."

"I don't want to get married." She simply said.

"What?!" Everyone chorused in disbelief.

"I want to get rid of this thing I am carrying inside." She told them.

She then heard something hitting her face.

It was a slap from Victoria. She didn't see it coming.

"If Em walked out and hesitant to slap you, I'm not. Now tell me you will not going to abort this child! Tell me, Casslynn!" Victoria shouted at her.

"Why did you slap me? I came here to ask your advice. You are my friends." She can't help but cry. Her face hurts.

"You cannot abort the child!" Shane said, words with deeper force.

"I didn't ask you to tell me what to do. This is my child, my body!" She shouted back at them. She felt upset now.

"Then I don't see why you need to see us, young woman." Adelaide, Jenna and Brenn left.

"I agree with the others." Victoria said.

So everyone left her.

And she felt even more miserable.

Chapter 36

Two years later...

"C'mon, Alexa. Hurry up, sweetie. We will get late."
He called his daughter who came back inside the house
trying to get her Barbie doll.

"Where's your dad?"

He heard Casslynn calling for him. He saw her
carrying Lexin Apollo. Lexin is their third child.

Two years ago when they discovered Casslynn was
pregnant for the second time they were both furious and
tried to plan to abort the child. They are both glad they
didn't.

"Oh there you are." She said when she saw him sitting
on the driver's side.

"Did we forget anything?" He asked her.

"I guess we have everything." She smiled.

Oh crap! There is one thing that didn't change in the past years, Casslynn's smile still make him grow hard. And every time Casslynn delivered another baby in the house she looked even more beautiful.

"I'll sit with Daddy." They heard Alexa.

"I want to sit with Mommy." Lexand said.

"No, sweethearts, both of you will sit with Daddy in the front seat. Lexin will stay with me here in the back seat. Do you understand?" Casslynn told them. Alexa pout and Lexand almost cried.

"Lex and Alexa can sit in front seat while the mommy can sit on daddy's lap taking care of his protruding big-"

"Pervert! Not in front of children, daddy!" She glared at him. He just smirked.

"Mom, what's pervert?" Alexa ask innocently.

"That's dad, sweetie and mom loves it when dad is pervert." He teased her.

"Alexis! Stop it and drive!" He could see her eyes glowing with anger and if she is a dragon she could blow up the entire car now.

He gave a loud laugh, confusing the children. "Mom is mad. Come." He carried his twins with him to the front seat.

Today is family day. Robert and Rowena invited them to stay in the resort for a week. The couple will go to Thailand for a week and they ask their help to watch over their three kids. In return, they will stay in the resort for a week as VIPs.

He felt cryptic with his own term. *'Family'*. Family is often associated with marriage. Casslynn and he are still not married. Though his friends did their best to convince him to marry Casslynn. He won't. It's good that he has Casslynn as the woman running the house, raising the kids, but having her as the woman who will give full control on everything not only his present and future but also his past is another thing. His parents in the States didn't even have any idea that he has three kids with Casslynn.

They arrive at Pentagon Knights after almost an hour. Lexand requested to carry him in his back when they get out from the car, so he did. Alexa also wanted her daddy to carry her and he did too. While Casslynn carry Lexin with her. So all their things were left in the car.

Ben meet them and was laughing at Alexis.

"You look good, bro! Few more children and would look better." His friend teased him. "Hey, Monica."

"Call me Casslynn, Ben." She told him while looking around. "Which one is our room? I really want to get rest now. This child is very heavy." Referring to Lexin Apollo.

"Mommy, down. I want swim." Her youngest child is trying to get free from her arms and looking at Rowena's kids swimming in the pool closer by.

"Not yet, sweetie." She tried to balance him in his arms.

"I asked someone to pick up your things in the car. We have prepared delicious and healthy food for you." Charlie arrived, smiling at her. "Hey, Casslynn, you look even great. Looks like having kids suit you better."

"Thank you, Charlie." She smiled at Alexis' friend.

"Charlie!" Alexis looks mad.

But Casslynn didn't see it as she was busy thinking of the food that the resort prepared for them.

"Ops. I didn't mean to make you jealous, bro."

"Stay back or else." He gave his friend a killer look.

"Excuse me, Sir, I thought you might want to check if we have all the things you need inside. If you have a second." A man approached him. He recognize him as one of their headwaiters.

"Why are you here? You are supposed to be in the restaurant." He glared at Ben. When Robert is not around sometimes the staffing arrangement of the resort is messed up.

"I could take care of the kids while you bring Casslynn inside to check your things." Ben said ignoring his glaring look.

"No, Alexis, can check our things. I want to eat.'

"No, leave the kids to Ben and you will come with me inside woman." Without a second Ben get Lexi from Casslynn's arm and the rest of the children followed him inside the restaurant.

"What is your problem?" Casslynn asked him when they were inside their cabin.

"My problem is this." He showed her his hard shaft.

"Shit, Alexis! You are not planning to fuck me here, are you?"

"A quickie, please, *ganda*." He sounded like begging but then he slide her skirt up and pulled down her panty. "I am glad you love wearing dresses instead of pants."

"Not anymore. Starting today I plan to wear pants."

"Oh, please. If you do that, I will have hard time inserting my big gun inside you."

"Exactly the point why I would want to wear a pants. Ah, shit." She didn't know she was wet, now it was very easy for Alexis to push his big shaft inside her.

"Ah, *ganda*, you never failed to make me crazy." He pushed deeper and faster. He didn't stop from there. He give little kisses to her neck before giving her a small bite which hurts a little.

"Shit! What do you think you're doing?"

"Putting you kiss mark so men out there would know that we made love and you are mine. Ah." He had her sit on a table now and still pushing harder inside.

"Alexiss, ah!"

"*Ganda*." He suck her breasts, placing her tongue from one nipple to another. "I am cumming!"

She wanted to push him. But it was too late he released his warm seed inside her.

Shit!

She cursed silently. Since her last pregnancy they practiced withdrawal. She cannot afford to get pregnant again. But she felt scared now. Today is not the first time that Alexis explode his sperm inside her, there had been a couple of times in the past month or two.

She prayed silently. Maybe, maybe not this time. She doesn't want to get pregnant again.

"You are very beautiful, *ganda*. As usual you always made me the most satisfied man in this world." He kissed her hard on the mouth. "Let's go to our children and feed your hungry stomach." He said, smiling.

She followed him, still trying to whisper a short prayer not to become pregnant again.

Chapter 37

"YOU can touch anything inside this house but this!"

She was doing some cleaning stuff inside the house when he saw some old albums in Alexis' drawer. Normally he would lock his drawer but today he left it open.

"I don't have any plan to look at it. I was just cleaning the house when I stumble into your things. You don't need to shout at me! I am not stupid!"

One week ago they returned home after staying at Pentagon Knights for a week. Since then Alexis had been in bad mood. He played with the kids but he is no longer as sweet as before, especially not to her.

"Don't ever touch my things again!"

"What's your problem? Since we returned home, you have been acting like stupid!?"

"Don't call me stupid! Yes, you are smart! You are beautiful! You are sexy! You look great even if you had already delivered three kids! Yes, you have it all for every man in this world to fall for you! Are you satisfied?!"

"Is this still about the compliment that Charlie gave me in the resort? Are you jealous with Charlie?"

"Jealous? Don't give me that fucking word! You are not even my girlfriend! Stop acting like one!"

She's hurt! But she's the type who doesn't easily surrender on a fight.

"Then why are you acting like one?"

"Shut up, Casslynn! I just need you to stop touching my things. Do you understand?"

"Daddy." Alexa was standing at his back.

"Are you fighting, Mommy?" Then Lex is standing on the door.

"Mommy. Daddy." Lexin is standing behind Lex.

"No, we are not." They both said it together. She glared at Alexis telling him to go.

"I need to go to work, Sweetie." He kissed Alexa, then Lex and Lexin. "I'm going to miss the three of you. Behave, okay?"

"Yes, daddy." The three kids said in chorus.

"I need to go." He just look at her before closing the door on her. That's it. No kiss, no hug. She seemed to be living with a new Alexis. She doesn't understand what's wrong with him.

Alexis, on the other hand, glance back at the house with a sad look.

How he wish Casslynn gave him kiss and hug before leaving. But he doubt if he wants her kisses and hug either.

Franky! That stupid man! Traitor! He wonder how many rounds did he and Casslynn had.

"Fuck! Fuck!" He shout inside the car before driving away.

He won't forget what happened back in the resort. Franky and Casslynn were together while he was busy taking care of the kids. Casslynn told him she needs to fix something in the city and she needs to go to LGP. He then realize he needs to pick up a mail in the city, too. There he saw Franky and Casslynn coming out from a hotel, they were both laughing, didn't even notice him.

"Fuck! How could you do this to me, Casslynn? I thought I made you satisfied enough! How could you sleep with another man? I never slept with another woman since I've met you! Fuck you!"

If this is USA he could be charged with over speeding now with the way he's driving.

He wants to kill someone. That asshole! Bastard friend of his! He knows that he is guilty of sleeping with his woman. He went out of the country on the same day he caught him and Casslynn together.

Casslynn, I thought you are different from among all women I met in life. But you are just like them. All of you women are the same. All of you are the same like Laura!

Shit! Shit! Shit!

Chapter 38

IT was the busiest day of her life. She was trying to finish one book while the kids are busy doing stuff. She bought lots of drawing and writing books for the kids. Also different sort of movies and music videos.

She will stop from writing her book after she heard her alarm ringing. She had to, otherwise she wouldn't notice that it's already meal time and she can't afford to get the kids hungry.

Alexis and she decided not to get a nanny because it would suit the kids best if their mother would personally take care of them. But she had an on-call nanny whenever there's something very important coming. Like now.

It's almost midnight and Alexis is still not home. It's the first time that he will come home late without notifying her.

She texted May to watch over the sleeping kids while she go look for Alexis.

She took a cab to Pentagon Knights.

She doesn't normally check on Alexis. She trust him that he won't do anything that could ruin their relationship, after all if it's sex he wants she never failed to satisfy him.

But tonight is different. Maybe because Alexis had been acting so different lately. And she knows that she's being very demanding again. She doesn't understand herself, too. She wants to see Alexis every day. Smell his scent. And the kids are looking for their father whenever he is not around.

Alexa had been asking her if she can see her dad again. Her daughter is very smart. She doesn't talk much but she observes and listens a lot, one thing that she's afraid of. Her daughter is very suspicious on everything. Doesn't easily trust on anyone other than her mother and father. Alexa is just like her, her younger version, only that she look very much exactly like her father. And her kind is the one who are always left out. Henry left her. Her parents and sister are dead, living her alone. And she doesn't want to happen it to Alexa or to any of her kids. She wants them to have a happy, wholesome family.

She reached the resort after 30 minutes. She paid the driver and hurriedly went inside the resort.

The security guard greeted her.

He saw Ben outside the bar talking to Robert. When they saw her, their faces went pale. She guessed Alexis is assigned to watch the counter tonight. Well, she doesn't really interfere with Alexis' life whether it be business or personal. She doesn't ask a lot, too.

"Casslynn! What are you doing here in this middle of the night? Where are the kids?" Robert greeted him but she can feel there's something else going on.

"I called May and had her watch the kids. They are all asleep. Where's Alexis? I'm worried."

"H-e already left. Yes, right. H-e must be on his way home now." Ben stuttered a little. She knows when a person lie or not.

"I know he's not. Is he with someone else? A woman? Where is he?" She's starting to get angry at his friends who are trying to protect Alexis.

"Ahm. I guess its better you go home, Casslynn. Alexis is drunk and-" She didn't let Robert finish talking. She get inside the bar.

And surely she saw Alexis, with a lady sitting on his lap. Maybe she's older than her. She looks sexy and tall. A woman of her opposite.

She is filled with rage when she approached them. Ben and Robert tried to stop her but she yelled at them.

She didn't pay attention to people inside the bar. Men are looking at her full of attraction. Women are looking at her full of envy. Why not, she's wearing her sleeping wear, and she look like a Goddess walking on earth.

"So, is this the reason why you didn't even texts me or call that you will come home late?"

Alexis turned sober all of a sudden after hearing Casslynn's voice.

"Casslynn? What are you doing here?" He asked with face full of guilt.

"Who is she?" The woman sitting on his lap looking at her from head to toe.

"You are asking my name? I'm Casslynn! And this guy here you are kissing with, is the father of three kids, our own kids. Now, I don't want anyone messing with my man because I hate to hurt my hands!" Without a second she grab the woman's hair. Slap her on the right and left face. She then punch her on the face before giving her a flying kick. The woman looks like a battered wife with blood all over her nose while she's trying to feel the pain of her kick in her stomach.

"Stop it, Casslynn!" Ben and Robert tried to take her away from the woman but she's very strong.

"Alexis, get your wife away from here! You will pay for causing this scandal! It's ruining our business." Robert is shouting at the Alexis who could not believe that Casslynn is capable of hitting a woman taller and bigger than her. She's 5'2 and the woman is about 5'8.

Casslynn felt Alexis grabbing her waist and carried her like a sack of rice before she was pushed to the passenger side of his car.

"I will kill that woman! I will kill her!"

"Shut up! Let me drive and we will talk when we get home!"

She hit him on the shoulder.

"How could you do this to me? You bastard! How many fucking rounds did you have with that woman! How many? Tell me!"

He didn't answer her. It's no use to talk to a mad woman.

"I said, tell me!"

"Will you please shut up? Shut up, Casslynn! If you will not stop, I will wring your neck! Do you understand me?"

She stop in awe.

Until they reached home, Casslynn didn't speak a word.

He was blown with madness soon as she opened the door.

"What do you think you are doing? You are making a great scandal in the resort! Do you know who that woman you attacked with punches and must be in the hospital now? Do you know who she is? She is the daughter of one of our major client in the resort! You just messed up with my business!"

"Oh, so is it part of your business now to kiss and fuck the daughter of your investor? Is that why you are acting like mad and stupid lately? You no longer want me for sex?"

"I can't believe you are acting like an uncivilized person, Casslynn!"

"So am I the one uncivilized now? What do you think you are doing, is it civil? Don't you remember you have me, you have kids waiting for you and you are there smooching other women?"

"Stop acting like you are my wife, because you are not even my girlfriend! You are just a fucking bed partner and mother to my kids!"

She slapped him.

"How dare you! How could you say that to me? What have I done that you have to treat me like a whore? Tell me!" She feel her hands go numb and too weak to slap and beat him, instead she let all the tears flow over her face.

"Do you want to know why? Because you are no longer the petite woman I wanted so much in bed! You have saggy breasts and loose vagina! Do you think you can still make me satisfied? And you are no longer the same woman with a beautiful face that every man in this world would want to die for!"

She gave him another slap. Before she burst into another tears.

"I should see this coming. Huh, everyone thinks of me as the smartest in my team. The most intelligent. And here I am became stupid because of you. I should know your type. I thought you are different, Alexis, you made me believe I could have the happy family I dreamed of. A man and husband who will never exchange me for another woman! You are just another asshole! Another asshole who deserves to rot in hell! I wish you will never find the happiness in your heart with another woman! That woman you just fucked in the bar? She will just leave you, exchange you to another man! And you will grow old alone!"

"What are you going to say next? You are leaving? And then what, you will demand money? I am not stupid to give you a penny!"

She smiled. A smile full of pain.

"Your money? Do you think that's what I am after for? I don't need a goddam cent from you! And yes, I am leaving. The kids will go with me!"

"Fine. I don't want to see your face in the morning! Make sure you won't leave even a little reminder of your existence inside my house."

She throw him some photos, a bank book and keys.

"Fuck! That hurts!"

She didn't say a word.

He saw her placing hers and the children's clothes inside a big traveling bag.

He wanted to stop her. But he didn't. What Franky and she did inside the hotel is something he can never forgive.

Chapter 39

"WHY are you not sleeping yet? And you are drinking again, son."

It's his father.

"What's the father and son doing at this hour outside the house, hmm?" His mother joined them.

He is back in his hometown in Minnesota, USA. He left the foreign country he considered his home country two months ago. He had a great battle with Robert before giving him the permission to leave.

"Don't you have any plan to go home? Remember, this is our business, not your home." Robert is indirectly throwing him out of their own bar.

"The house is empty, Rob. I have no more wine in my keeping. I wish I have a wine cellar." He smiled, a very sad smile.

"It's no longer my concern, Alexis. You made a big mistake. I already told you before, Casslynn is a treasure but you still lost her."

It's been almost two weeks since Casslynn left with the kids. And two days ago he had a big confrontation with Franky. The asshole didn't even deny that he was with Casslynn inside the hotel.

"I don't want a woman who was tasted already by another man!" He said before he emptied another glass of wine.

"That wine costs 300 per glass." Robert reminded him. "And I have to remind you the costs of casualty damaged by Casslynn when she was here. I still need more power of words to convince that old man to invest in our resort after Natalia was battered by your wife."

That's it! He had enough of Robert McCarthy's lectures.

"What the fuck are you trying to say? That I am ruining our business? Am I not part of this business? Am I not supposed to contribute to the failure and success of this business?" He was shouting at Robert.

"What do you think you are doing, Alexis? Why are you blaming people for your misfortunes?" It was Franky. He arrived with a sexy woman clinging in his arms. "Go to my cabin, sweety, I am just going to deal with this madman."

"Oh the asshole! The traitor is here!" He give him a big punch on the face. To which Franky accepted and throw him back with another bigger, stronger punch. Ben and Charlie tried to stop the two from fighting. Robert is just watching. He knows the whole story. Franky told him everything.

"What is your problem? You, Alexis, you already overstayed here! And you Franky, you just came back from your trip. And both of you are causing yet another trouble and scandal in this resort!" Charlie is very furious.

"Huh! This man? You consider a friend? Is a traitor!"

"Stop making up stories! If you are mad because Casslynn left with the kids, that's not our problem anymore!"

"I am not making up stories. I saw you with Casslynn coming out from the hotel. You are busy laughing with my woman you didn't even see me standing in front of your car! Assshole!"

"Oh that? Too bad, you caught us. Casslynn, is very beautiful, and yummy, you know. No one can even guess she already had three kids."

"Fuck you, Franky! I will kill you!" He wants to strangle him again but Ben is holding his arms very tight.

"No, thanks. I'd rather fuck, Casslynn!" He smirked even with blood on the nose.

"I will kill you! Let me go, Ben, I want to kill that bastard!"

"Fix your business partner, Robert, before I will schedule an appointment with the Insane Asylum." He said before leaving.

"Now you know how the pain hurts. You must have idea now how Casslynn felt when she saw you kissing with Natalia sitting on your lap." Ben said.

"But I wasn't sleeping with that woman. I may have kissed her out of alcohol influence but I didn't fuck her and you all know that. I never slept any woman since I had Casslynn." He said feeling more miserable. He look miserable too, he can feel his beard growing, no time to shave his mustache.

"I don't know what to do with you." Ben said, showing his surrender. "I guess Charlie and Robert can help." He said before leaving him.

"I have done my part." Charlie said before leaving, too.

"Are you going to leave me, too?" He asked Robert when he saw him staring at him.

"*What is it that you are so mad about? Is it Casslynn you saw with Franky inside the hotel? Or is it Casslynn and the kids leaving you alone in a big house?*"

"*You don't understand me, Rob. I don't want any man to sleep with Casslynn. She's mine. Just mine!*"

"*She's not married to you. Technically, she is not yours.*"

"*She's mine. She deliver my kids. She's living with me! What difference that does make?*"

"*Do you love Casslynn?*"

"*Why should that matter?*"

"*Do you know that I am scared to get married as well? But when I met Rowena, I want her mine. And the only way to do that is to marry her. There is a big difference in wanting a woman because of sex and wanting a woman because you love her.*"

"*You don't understand. I can't marry her.*"

"*This is not a question of you wanting to marry her or not. But the fact that you let her go, hurt her. Slap the words in her face that she's just a sex partner, that her uterus is just a factory of your babies. Any smart woman would understand what you want. Stop being miserable. Go on with your life. This is what you want after all. Be single forever? Then be it. Don't mess your personal life with our business.*"

"*I can't.*" He said before Robert can turn his back on him. He fell on her knees crying. "*I hate the sound of silence. I hate that there are no kids running and crying inside the house. I hate that I have no woman in my arms when I'm both happy and sad. I hate being alone.*" He told him the story of his past.

"*Casslynn didn't sleep with Franky. Casslynn is not the same as the women you regularly meet. I bet she would even prefer to die than being touched by a man other than you. You should know that.*"

"*I saw her with Franky coming out from the hotel.*"

"*I believe you. But did you check what Casslynn did inside the hotel? She was trying to follow-up the registration of your children in the National Statistics Office. Because you never have time to do it yourself. If there is anyone who knows your personal information that would be us. Only Franky was available at that time.*"

"*What? You're saying that-*"

"*Precisely. You were jealous on nothing.*"

"*God!*"

"*So sad, you have hurt and insulted Casslynn so much because of your wrong assumptions and accusations.*"

"*God! Casslynn... My children... So stupid of me.*"

"*I agree.*"

"*What am I going to do now?*"

"*What do you want to do now?*" Robert look at his eyes.

"*I want Casslynn back and our kids. I love her.*"

"*And what else?*"

He just stared at his friend.

"*I don't know.*"

"*You know. How about you take a vacation? Go back to your hometown. Face Laura. See your kid with her. If you can't move on with your past, how are you going to face the present and future with Casslynn?*"

"*Do you think that's a good idea?*"

"*Yes.*" Then Robert went to the counter to answer a call but he gave him another word. "*When you see Casslynn again, don't let your emotions decide for you, bro. Learn to listen. The lesser you talk but the more you listen will clear out the situation. Casslynn is a good listener. I would say she would never make a wrong decision.*"

"*She left with the kids. Do you think that's a good decision?*"

"She didn't. She's in her apartment, you know that. She's waiting for you to make a decision that could change both of your lives."

Robert is right. Casslynn is in her apartment with the kids.

"The reason you join with me in this business is to get a reward right? Well, then this is the prize, bro. A happy family for you."

"You, idiot!" His mother spank his butt.

"Stop it, mom. That hurts!"

"I would want to strangle you if only you are not my son!" His father seemed to be siding with his mother.

"How could you hide us our own grandchildren? Two years, Alexis Isaiah and you told us just now about the kids and Casslynn? What are you thinking?"

"I got scared, Ma, of all things. There's my past with Laura. I thought she will turned up like Laura. I hate to be controlled. I hate a nagging woman."

"Son, not all woman are like Laura. This Casslynn, I think she's a great woman, I think we would like her. What do you think hon?" His mother just nodded with agreement. "But being a nagger I guess it's natural to women."

"I don't know what to do, Pop."

"What does your heart tells you, son?"

"I want Casslynn. I want the kids. I want a happy family."

"Well, go and get your family back, Son. We are excited to see our grandchildren and welcome Casslynn in our family."

"I'm leaving tomorrow, Ma, Pop."

"Let me buy you a ticket, Son."

"Make it three, Ma. You will travel with me. I want to raise my kids in Andromeda not here."

"If you give us few days to make arrangements with our business here."

He smiled at his parents.

He is excited to see Casslynn and his children again.

Chapter 40

"MOMMY, hurry up, someone's ringing the doorbell!"

Her daughter Alexa is shouting to the top of her lungs. She's having hard time moving around the house with three kids. She can't work on her books very well. It's really hard taking care of three kids alone. And it's even harder now that she is pregnant.

Yes, she's pregnant of Alexis' fourth child. And she knows if Alexis would see her now, he will laugh at her looks. She's a little bit thin compared to her previous pregnancy. She has little black circles around her eyes due to lack of sleeping. She can't eat well due to her change of appetite. She tied up her hair in a ponytail style. She hardly had time to comb her hair or look at her face in the mirror. In short, she's completely ugly. Alexis must be fucking beautiful women now. Ah the typical womanizer as he is.

"Mommy, Alexa went outside. She's opening the gate!" Lexand shout.

Shit!

Alexa is the type who will tell you to do something but if you cannot do it fast, she cannot wait and she will do it for you instead. Her daughter got that attitude from her.

"Alexaaa! Lexand, wait here. And fix your things sweetie, please." She run through the gate carrying Lexin with her. She cannot leave Lexin with Lexand alone or the two will just fight to death.

She cannot see Alexa on the gate. It made her sick. Her daughter just opened their gate to a stranger.

"Mommy." Someone called from her back. It was Alexa. When she turned she was surprised to see who's carrying her daughter.

The man seemed to be growing in years. He has beard all over his face. His mustache grow. He looks like not able to shave for months.

"What are you doing here? I didn't give you the permission to visit my children! Put down, Alexa. Go, help your brother fixing your books."

"Our children!" He said.

"Really? When did you realize you have children?!" She felt a little pain in her stomach. She doesn't want to get upset.

"You're, you're pregnant?" She thought she saw a glimpse of joy in his eyes. But too much with her assumptions. It hurt so much when she assumed before that he wants her for keeps.

"I don't see any reason why you should be here. If you are thinking of the money I spent from your pocket, I didn't spend them for myself but for the children. Don't worry I am working very hard to pay you back."

"Give Lexin to me, he is very heavy. You should not be carrying our baby or any heavy things when you are pregnant."

"Stop playing games with me, Alexis. Tell me what you want and leave!"

"Daddy. Mommy." They forget that Alexa is still there looking at them. Crying.

"Sweetie." Alexis hug and kiss her daughter. If they are not a difficult situation she must have leaped with joy by the way he cared for their own daughter.

"I thought you told me you are not leaving us again." Her daughter cried.

"Hush, sweetie. I am telling you the truth. I love you. I love Lexand and Lexin. You are my life. You see, daddy is living a very miserable life when you, your brothers and your mom are not around."

"Promise?"

"Promise, sweetie. Now, if you can bring Lexin with you inside, I want to talk to your mom. Okay?"

"Okay, Daddy. Come on, Lexin," Alexa guide her younger brother inside and she is left with Alexis.

Soon as Alexa came inside, Alexis hugged and kissed her. If she was the same woman who let her heart rule rather than her head, maybe, she would believe him.

"Let me go!"

"No! I missed you so much, *ganda*." He hugged her, didn't give her the chance to go.

But sometimes when she's angry she has this unusual strength. When she was finally free from his arms, she give him a slap.

Alexis' face grow red. She swear she saw a hand mark on his face.

"Stop calling me that. My fantasies are over. Don't you see it? Not only that I have saggy breasts and loose vagina, I am ugly all over!"

She saw hurt in his eyes. And was that tears he's trying to stop from falling? No, she's just assuming things again.

"I'm sorry. I didn't mean to say it. I was mad. Furious with jealousy."

She can't help but cry.

He is trying to touch her face to wipe away the tears.

"Don't touch me, Alexis. Whatever you said to me back there in Andromeda, it changed me. You made me lost my self-confidence. The only thing I had for myself, my pride, I lost it, too. You insulted my female being. You forgot I delivered three kids that by all means, would change my physical female being. I felt totally dirty."

She saw him crying. It is not her imagination anymore. But looks can be deceiving, it could be that Alexis was an actor in his past life. She just realized she didn't really know this man. Aside from his real name, age, address and birthday, she know nothing of this man. His parents, his origin.

"I am hurt by what I said to you. I know you won't believe me, but my life was never the same when you left with the kids. I want you back, *ganda*, please give me the chance."

"I only trust a man once, Alexis. Just once and if it fails I cannot trust the same man again. You break my trust. There is nothing you can do to fix it."

"Please, *ganda*, swear to heavens I will do everything. And I don't want you to go through this pregnancy alone. I want to be there again, every step of the way."

"Everything?"

He went pale but still managed to give her an answer. "Y-yes."

"You know what I want, Alexis. You know my dream. I want marriage."

He turned even paler this time, not able to speak a word.

"Oh, yeah. What would I expect from you anyway?" Another single tear fall from her eyes. "I will tell the kids they can see you one day. Close the gate when you leave." She slam the door on him.

Shit!

It was too late for him to realize that Casslynn is closing the door on him. Fuck! He is not going to lose her and the kids again, is he?

He called his parents from the States and told them to fly on that day. And he sent a message to his friends and the women of LGP.

'Help me plan a very memorable proposal for Casslynn. I am going to marry her.'

Chapter 41

S HE opened the door for Shane and Victoria that early evening. Sadie Bryce and Kenne Jay were with them, too. These two were officially part of Team Jewels since a month ago. She was surprised to see them. She knows that everyone is busy but her friends still remembered her.

"Goodness! You look awful." Victoria's first comment when she see her.

"Don't worry, Mommy Vic, we can fix Ms. Monica." Kenne said. "Right, Sadie?"

"I can turn her into a goddess but I bet you can only turn Ms. Monica into a monster. So no, thanks!?"

She laughed. As usual these two are always fighting. But she can see that they look good together. A brilliant idea came into her mind. She will write these two a book.

'A Gay Meets The Looking Gay'. It's perfect. She wanted to smile. But she can't.

"I know. The pregnancy doesn't really suit me well, I guess." She told Victoria with sad look.

"And what's wrong with your eyes? Were you crying whole night, Casslynn?" Shane said with disbelief.

"A bit. He was here two days ago. I thought he's coming for me and the kids, you know for keeps. But I was wrong." She cried again.

"Hush. It's not good for the baby if you will keep doing this. You cannot always cry, that would affect your baby's health." Victoria said.

"What do you want me to do? Laugh because Alexis got me pregnant with his fourth child yet he still doesn't want to marry me?"

"No." Victoria turned to Shane. "Could you make an emergency call and call him?"

"Who's him? Alexis? Don't!"

"Silly, no, we have a new boss. Go, Shane, make a call and make the appointment earlier than scheduled. Leave him no choice."

"Wow! Who's boss? Em didn't tell me anything."

"Of course, our new boss, can't resist my beauty. Now, let's get inside and fix the kids."

"Why? Are we going somewhere?"

"Just Shane, Sadie, Kenne and the kids. You will go with me."

"What's going on? Are you ladies hiding something from me?"

"Yes. Our new boss. He is throwing up a party for everyone."

"Alright. It's settled. Now, we will take care of the kids and you will take care of Casslynn."

"I'm tired. You know that I am a party spoiler. I will just fall asleep there."

"It's closer to my place. So now, Monica, I need you to follow as I say." The authoritative tone of Victoria. She then followed as she's told. It's making her exhausted to argue with her.

Victoria told her to get some shower first. She hates taking a bath, she feel cold. But this woman is forcing her.

It took her five minutes only to finish her shower.

"Wow! So fast. Are you sure you put on some shampoo?"

"Silly. Of course. Smell me."

"Hmm, I believe you. Now, wear this." She hand her a paper bag with a pink dress. She wear it. She looked sexy and beautiful. But her bare shoulders are exposed and a little of her cleavage.

"This dress is beautiful, but it's revealing. Can I wear something else?"

"Ah uh, you can't. Now, sit here and let me fix your face though I don't think it needs more fixing. I guess a little powder, eye shadow, blush on and lipstick would do."

"Why do I need to put on those?"

"Don't argue with me, okay?"

"Can you also dry my hair using the dryer?" She didn't tell her that she likes the hair dryer because it's making her sleepy.

"Sure. I guess, let's dry your hair first and do your hair later." After few minutes she fell asleep.

Perfect, Casslynn. I cannot do what I plan if you are awake.

She went fast asleep. Victoria enjoyed her short sometimes long breathing.

You owe me a lot, Alexis.

When Casslynn wakes up. She was alone. But she was amazed of her look in the mirror.

She's beautiful. Really, her pregnancy is making her ugly. But now she's transformed.

She heard someone walking. It was Victoria, in her high-heeled shoes. If she's not pregnant she could wear one of those.

"Are you ready?" Victoria asked her. She gave her a rose flower-designed flat shoes.

"How do I look?"

"You look perfect! My boss would really appreciate your beauty."

"Does this new boss knows that I am pregnant?"

"Of course. Now, let's go."

"I need to see if the kids are okay."

"No, they are okay, Cass. Trust me, the kids are safe with their three nannies tonight. And they left two hours ago when you were asleep."

"I slept that long?"

"Yes, beauty. Now, let's go as the car is waiting outside."

Chapter 42

"WHY here?"

She may have fallen asleep again because the next thing she saw was the logo of Pentagon Knights. Victoria didn't answer her.

"Here's the headwaiter. He will guide you to the party, Cass. I need to park the car properly. I will see you inside."

"Wait, Victoria-" But she's gone. Must be to the parking area of the resort.

"Hello, Maam. They are waiting for you inside." It's the same headwaiter who assisted her and Alexis during her last stay in the resort.

"Who are they?"

The headwaiter only smiled at her. Guide her inside. And she was stunned to see many people inside the pavilion. She didn't know that Pentagon Knights had this very beautiful pavilion.

She recognize many faces. People from LGP. Writers from other publishing company. Of course she saw her JEWELS team. And Alexis' friends, Robert, Ben, Franky and Charlie. May her former on-call Nanny was there, too. She was looking for a particular face. But she can't see him. She then realize, Alexis is not a party goer either so she cannot really see him here.

"Mommy." She saw her kids calling her in chorus.

She smiled at them. Her daughter and sons look pretty and handsome tonight. Alexa looks gorgeous in her pink princess dress. Her daughter will grow up very beautiful, too bad Alexis will not be there for her. Lexand is very manly in his small tuxedo. And Lexin Apollo is cute with his white tuxedo. She can feel her tears are about to fall. If only Alexis witness this, he would know how adorable their kids are.

"Mommy, you are very beautiful." Lexand told her when she approaches the table where her kids are sitting.

"Hello, Casslynn. I expected you to be beautiful, but my goodness, you are more than beautiful. No wonder my grandkids are very handsome and pretty."

"And she's sexy, honey, just like you when you are still younger."

She was stunned. Who are these senior people giving her compliment?

Alexa must have read her mother's thoughts.

"Mommy, meet granny Lesley and grandpa Jordan."

"We are very happy to finally meet you, sweetie." The Lesley her daughter is talking about gave her a kiss and a hug from the senior man named Jordan.

She's not sure what to say. She didn't know that she has foreign fans as well. She just keep quiet. When a song was heard. It was a song from Chicago, 'You're the Inspiration'. A man was singing it from somewhere.

She always wanted to have Alexis sing it for her. Only that she never get the chance to ask him. It isn't really a very beautiful song, but it was Alexis' favorite. She can't help but cry when the man singing it almost finished the song. She remembered Alexis. She could guessed it's almost nine in the evening. Where is Alexis now? Ah he must be sleeping with another women! She sobbed. She really cannot accept the fact that Alexis cannot be faithful to her. She hates the idea of him sleeping with another woman.

She was distracted by the man speaking. Could he be speaking from her back? Ah she doesn't care. She only cares for one man.

"I want to thank all people who helped. My four pentagon brothers. The ladies from LGP, especially Victoria and Shane. How you convince her to attend this party I have no idea. Most of all, I appreciate my parents full support. This is what you get when you decided to settle down at a late age, you need everyone's help or else your proposal would turn out a mess and she may say no."

Everyone laugh, except her.

Did she just heard him mentioning Victoria's name? She may have heard it wrong.

"Of course, I want to appreciate my jewels, Alexa, Lexand and Lexin that they cooperate with their Auntie Shane."

Now, she is not hearing it wrong. The guy mentioned her kids' names.

She turned back and was shocked to see the man behind the microphone.

Alexis!

"Hello, *ganda*. I know I was stupid. I hurt you and I wish there is one thing I can do to take back all the words of insults I gave you that day. I was jealous of Franky or any man. You are mine and just mine. I was a coward for admitting my real feelings. I love you. I guess since the day I met you in FindSome. You were never erased here." He refers to his mind. "And here." He point his finger to his heart.

She only stared at him. Trying to ask him something. *What are you doing?*

When she look at the people around her, some were smiling, some were crying. Em was crying. Her kids are smiling. Even Alexa cheered for her father.

"Go, Daddy!"

"I know I break your trust. There is no way I can fix that again. I don't need you to trust me again. Just love me. Because if there's one thing I want in this life, it's your heart. Without you. Without the kids. I'm like an empty shell, *ganda*."

She remained silent. Tears flowing her face.

"I really hate to see you crying. I swear to heaven tonight is the last night I am going to make you cry." Now he is slowly walking towards her. And she is not stupid not to know what he is holding in his left hand. It's a ring!

"I know you told me about your dream and I told you mine. I'm one hell of a coward, I guess. I always thought you are mine, only mine. Until I'm knock into my senses that without marriage you are not officially mine. I don't want to marry you for the sake of marriage. I want to marry you because I want to keep you and our family. I love you. I have always wanted to tell you that. When you asked me the other day I was about to propose. But I guess I got scared again. But today, I should face my fear. It's marrying you or nothing at all. My *ganda,* the beautiful mother of my children, will you spend your lifetime with me? Will you marry me?"

He kneeled before her. Just like the kind of proposal she dreamed. Alexis is an image of a handsome knight.

"*Ganda*, please? Don't say no."

"Promise you won't hurt me again? You won't sleep with another woman again? Only me until your last breath?"

"I love you and I promise."

"Yes!"

"Alright, everyone you heard her say yes, okay? Now, I want to be married to this woman tonight."

Everyone clapped. Victoria came to her and unpinned the back part of her dress. She didn't know it was a gown.

The two seniors who kissed and hugged her earlier came forward, smiling at her.

"Maybe you wanted to formally introduce Casslynn to us, son." The old man named Jordan said smiling at Alexis. She saw how Alexis blushed.

"Ahm, *ganda*, I want you to meet my parents. This is my mom, Lesley Angela and my pop, Jordan. They are just dying to meet you."

She almost burst into tears when the two seniors hugged her again.

"Hello, sweetie. Call me Mom." Lesley said.

"And call me Pop, sweetie." Jordan said.

She gave each seniors a tight hug and a sweet smile.

She caught a glimpse of the sky. Thought she saw her parents and sister smiling up there. Then Destiny's rhyming words came back to her.

'The sun will go down and meet the moon, stars will be shown. One day, the sun will go away. What will matter is your laughter. Tear will always be there, but never fear as for you will be a happy ever after.'

It's ironic that all of sudden she understands what those words mean. She is the moon, Alexis is the sun. Her children are the stars. Alexis left her. There were pain and tears that both she and Alexis suffered. And here they are happy in each other's arms.

Jenna stared at her smiling and mouthed "*I told you*". She's referring to Destiny's rhyme prophecy. The priest show up and started the wedding ceremony.

Chapter 43

IT was their honeymoon night. Because she has been worn out entertaining the visitors and it's late in the evening, Casslynn decided to just spend the honeymoon in the resort.

They get to the penthouse Robert had reserved for them. The kids spent the rest of the nights with their grandparents. Casslynn was surprised to meet his parents but very happy.

He go past her while she close the door.

As she locks the door he grab her and take her gown off and pin her against the wall.

He moves her hair to her right side as he moves in closer to her neck and ear.

He bet, Casslynn can feel his breath, sending shivers through her spine.

He kissed her neck and behind her ear. Nibbling on her earlobe, with his tongue gently flick it. A small moan escapes her lips. He then put a finger over her mouth in a shushing way.

"Do you like this?" He whispered.

She replied a yes through her slight moan.

He kissed her neck again, moving her hair over and kissing the right side of her neck.

He take their shoes off and carried her to their bedroom. He slowly put her on the bed. She's naked from the top. He bent over and kiss the back of her neck again and go lower down her back. Reaching the top of her panty, he slowly pull it down.

"I have a sagging breast and loose vagina." She said, reminding him of his insulting words before. It made him stop from smooching her.

"That is not true either. I was stupid to say that. I love your cherry *my wife*. I love to watch your tummy swelling with my baby. I love you. Please forgive me."

"I love you, too, yummy. Now, taste me. And I forgave you already."

He can feel her wetness. He placed one finger, but then thought that it might hurt his baby, he take away the finger and move his tongue closer to 'her' lips. He licked from the bottom, right, between and up.

"I need your finger and tongue work together, yummy."

He did as told.

Now with a finger inside her playing with her gspot, his tongue joins in the fun. He heard her moan starts to become louder. By now, he got a full hard boner inside his pants. He pulled out his big gun. Tease her by putting his big gun between her legs and play around, just teasing her a little bit.

He lift her to face him right back.

He kissed her neck again, moving lower to her collarbone.

He could see her body shake while his right hand is going down to one of her breasts. Squeeze it a bit. Letting her feel his warm hand.

He then move his lips to the right breast, round the bottom and to the side. He did the same with the left breast but with his left hand remained on the right breast continue squeezing it, playing with the nipple. With his tongue go in a circulation movement getting closer and closer to her nipples. Biting them ever so slightly. Putting his whole mouth around her breast and sucking it like a baby, while playing with her nipple with his tongue.

He moved down to her ribs and stomach. He kissed her swelling belly.

"Hello my baby. Daddy is so excited to see you."

"Yummy, I'm so wet. Please stop talking."

"Yes, wifey." He moved her to the side with her ass facing her big gun. He thrusts slowly.

"Oh, shit. Deeper, baby."

It was in a slow motion. Then he fully thrusts his big gun inside her. He fuck her from the side. Her moan becomes louder and louder. Screaming his name.

Every thrusts, every push, Casslynn shouts his name. And he loves to listen to her sweet voice screaming his name.

When he completely explode inside her, he saw how she rolled her eyes with orgasm.

"I love you, my wife." He told her after releasing his warm seed inside her.

"I love you, too, my husband."

He let her rest in his arm.

"Are you happy?" He asked her while stroking her hair.

"Very happy."

"Can you forgive me for hurting you?"

"Of course. It's enough that you asked forgiveness, loving me and the kids."

"Thank you. Ma and Pop are so happy to meet you finally. And I guess it's time I told you about Laura."

"Hmmm. I want to listen."

"I spent a year with her before I kicked her out and told her never to come back. It was after that she threw things I had since childhood. Including the old album you touched before. She did anything and everything she could to hurt me. I would wanted to marry her and father my kid, but I can't take her attitude anymore. And it scared me to marry a woman like her."

"I am not like Laura. And I'm the kind who value old memories so much."

"I know that wife. Those photos you threw at my face before, those were photos taken when I have not even met you, but you got them printed."

"True, 'cause I valued our friendship so much."

"Thank you. And I guess it's time you should know my family background. Why I have friends like Robert,

Ben, Charlie and Franky. How we became friends and a lot." He started to tell her his family origin. His businesses. His friendship with the rest of the knights from Pentagon.

She was speechless.

"You are saying that-"

"Wifey, you are married to a millionaire's son." He simply smiled. "And now I entrust you my entire finances. You are my boss, my bestfriend, my everything. I am giving you full control of me. And I mean you controlling my present, future and past. I love you so much for giving me beautiful children."

THE END

EPILOGUE

TWELVE YEARS LATER...

SHE tease 'him. Suck 'him'.

"Wife *ganda*, I want you to sore me. Please."

After all these years, finally Casslynn will make his dream come true.

"Beg, Alexis."

"I'm begging you wife *ganda*."

They just finished the second round of their lovemaking today. The kids are out with their grandparents. He is alone with Casslynn.

"I like your balls, yummy. They are heavy yet beautiful." She is holding his balls in her left hand. In her right is a thick brochure of a clothing company. She slapped her balls using the brochure. He could almost shout with pain. Sure that hurts. He could see that his balls now turned into a reddish color. She slapped it again. And yet another small voice of pain echoed inside the bedroom.

"Are you sure about this?"

"Yes, *my wife*. We have twelve children already and I am old."

Yes, twelve children! The third pregnancy that Casslynn had turned out to be triplets. All boys. Next was a girl. Then they had another doubles on the fifth pregnancy. Another boys again. The next sixth and seventh pregnancy were boys too. Finally, their youngest is a girl. Yet, he is still the same horny man. Never tired of making love with Casslynn. And Casslynn. She never grew tired of him either. Though most of the time Casslynn is a dominant woman. She's the last say in the house. Her words, her rule. He loves her even more. And now he's asking her to castrate him.

"Silly. You are not old yet. Old people can't fuck."

"That's why I love you so much, you don't really look at my age."

"Well, you are turning 56. Let me ask you again. Are you sure about this?"

She prepared the cutter.

"A bit nervous but I am ready."

"Alright. Spread your legs. Let me tie your balls first. Suck it before cutting them. Or do you want me to sore them first?"

Sure enough. She tied his balls very tight using a shoelace. It hurts like hell but the pain is satisfying.

She slap it again with the same brochure. From being reddish it now turned into almost as red as the fire.

"I love that! Argh! Wifey it hurts so much."

"Don't ask me to stop, because I won't!" She is saying it very sexy that he is having hard on again.

She suck each ball. When she's done, she clip it from the root. She could see him screaming with pain.

"Scream my name louder, husband. Scream."

"Casslynnnnn!"

It only took her few minutes to cut his balls.

"Yummy, you are now castrated."

He didn't speak a word, she thought he died.

"Thank you, *ganda*."

"Your balls are big. Let me wash them first. I have prepared a good place to preserve them."

He saw her going to the bathroom.

Fuck! His thigh and between really hurt. He could see the blood flowing all over the bed. But it's great.

He saw her coming back. She carried with her a transparent glass. It's probably one ruler tall. The glass is filled with water. But there is a layer of different jelly bean candies in the bottom.

"Now, I will put your castrated balls inside this glass and let it sit on top of the jelly bean candies."

She did as she said it.

"Then I will put this inside the fridge, making sure this will get frozen in a few days. And on your birthday, I will proudly show them to our friends. What do you think?"

"That's perfect, *my wife!* But do you think I could walk in a few days?"

"Sure you can."

*****

On Alexis' birthday, instead of cake, what was on top of the main table is his frozen balls inside a transparent glass.

"I can't believe you did it, bro." Robert exclaimed.

His friends know that it has been his dream to be castrated by a woman. Luckily, she happens to be his wife.

"And it seems like a dream. The man who was once a womanizer, too scared to have a kid or tying the knot, now have kids not one but twelve of them. I am very proud of you, bro!" Ben said while laughing out loud.

Ben only had three kids with Maridelle. While Robert also have three with his wife. While Charlie and Franky's wives are currently pregnant with their fourth children.

"I'm very proud of my wife. Now, even if a naked woman will try to touch my big birdie inside 'he' will no longer get hard. Only my wife can make 'him' hard."

"Now, let's' ask the pretty Alexa." Ben asked Alexis' eldest daughter.

"I am proud of Daddy, he loves Mom so much that he lets her cut his balls."

"And Lexand?"

"It's creepy and I feel nervous. But I think I want to be castrated by my wife someday, too. What do you think, Dad?"

"Oh my big boy. I would want you to experience it. But first find a woman with your mom's look, attitude and talents." Alexis told his son.

"I guess I found her, dad." Every one of them look at the teenage girl who run with her two-piece. With sexy butt and amazing breasts.

And they burst out laughing. Except Casslynn.

"My goodness, Lexand Casseus, you are not going to inherit your father's womanizing skill, are you?"

"I want to be pervert like Dad. Didn't Dad say you like it more when he is pervert?"

Alexis just laugh at his wife, now ready to blow fires at him.

"Alexis, I need you to teach your son good manners! I mean it! Now!"

As obedient as he is, Alexis scolded Lexand. His friends laugh at him. But when Casslynn wasn't paying attention he teach his son techniques on how to make a woman fall for a man.

Lexand just proudly told his father.

"I just want to be like you dad. I want to meet a beautiful writer too, who will give me awesome orgasm and castrate me later on."

The rest of the men inside the room salute the handsome duplicate copy of Alexis Isaiah.

ACKNOWLEDGMENT

I appreciate the help and support of my Check-In Coordinator, Ram Gregory, and the endless effort of my Publishing Services Associate, J.G. Elas. To the rest of the Earl Thomas' team, good job.

I would like to mention special people who played great role in my life for years now. If Snow White has 7 dwarfs who became her companion until she met her Prince Charming, I have lovely writers, not seven but nine of them I considered my best friends and sisters. To the beautiful moms from GEMS, to the pretty Editor who lead the group, Mommy Jiah, thank you for the inspiration. It's been a long battle to fight with you ladies but I appreciate you for giving me the permission to write for iUniverse.

I acknowledge the special participation of Kenn and Mercy Joy. It's a pride to include you in my story.

To the following people, my friends, who enjoy reading romance books and appreciate the works of authors: Shuegarr, Dhesney, Mandy, Carlos, Melaine, Sara Lou, Shiela M., Rowella, Reah, Sheryl, Andi, J. Raven and others, thank you.

To my cousins Rusty and GM, who are making collections of works from GEMS and sister imprints, another additional to your collections. Thank you.

To my sisters who became my first fans when my first book was released in print: Lou, Anj and Juliet. Thank you for trusting my skill.

A special acknowledgment of a friend who designed my book cover. I know how it shocked you when you first saw my book cover. I appreciate you for spending hours to work on my cover mock ups. Adriel Kaye, thank you so much.

Lastly, my inspiration in writing this book, Matthew Andersen, I owe you a lot. A heartfelt thanks for being there with me, for your trust. Thank you for your support, you embolden me to write this book. Thanks for sharing your life story and creating a fiction out of it. Our friendship is like the sky, just look up, it's infinite and never ending.

ABOUT THE AUTHOR

"*L*ooks can be deceiving", an old adage goes. So beware...

SANDRA ATHENA is a simple person with big dreams for her family and none for herself but true love. Started writing at the age of thirteen where she was appointed as the Editor-in-chief for their school paper until she graduated in highschool. It's her business to know the life story of her friends and put it into writing. It's her joy to see people reading her books without knowing her real identity. Other than romance, she had been writing horror, suspense and fantasy stories. She writes by heart and this will be her first romance book written in full English.

Printed in the United States
by Baker & Taylor Publisher Services